WHERE FLEMISH DREAMS ARE MADE

Enjoy
Lucian

WHERE FLEMISH DREAMS ARE MADE

LUCIEN FIRMAN CATTRYSSE

IGUANA

Copyright © 2024 Lucien Firman Cattrysse
Published by Iguana Books
720 Bathurst Street
Toronto, ON M5S 2R4

Publisher: Cheryl Hawley
Editor: Paula Chiarcos
Front cover design: Jonathan Relph

ISBN 978-1-77180-713-5 (paperback)
ISBN 978-1-77180-714-2 (epub)

This is an original print edition of *Where Flemish Dreams Are Made.*

To my mother, Justine Cattrysse, whose love and support made homecomings from travel feel very special.

PROLOGUE
ANOTHER LIFE

Baldwin and Yvonne spoke softly to each other as they sat on a bench overlooking the narrow canal outside of Damme. It was four in the morning. A half moon provided enough light to see the slight rippling of the slowly flowing waters. They shared the quiet night, interrupted every few minutes or so by a cricket chirping a rhythmic protest. Or perhaps it felt their thoughts.

The chirping stopped, as if in answer, giving them that minute of silent respite, each to their own feelings.

"I see you," he said.

"And I see you," she replied.

He picked up her hand, held it in his, briefly gave it a squeeze and put it down in her lap.

"We each need another life," she said.

PART 1

RELEASE

Baldwin van Ryssel, in his haste heading out the door, almost tripped over the family bouvier, Leopoldje, who was stretched out in the morning sun that was spilling through the kitchen windows of the cottage. He had just been reading his favourite battered text, *The Crusades 1000–1200*, which he left on the small shelf near his bedside. Heading out of the small garden with a skip in his step, he waved hello to his elderly neighbour, who was bent over a hoe in a patch of leeks, onions and cabbage, carefully tended to maximize the bounty of her small corner of the polder. He followed a short lane along the Vaart Canal, past the towering windmill and, rounding a corner, he soon found himself in the tightly cobbled town square of Damme, with its neat row of shops with peaked and stepped gable frontages in the Flemish style. His favourite view was of the ornate town hall with its quaint little carillon tower of twenty-five bells. It was largely blocked that day, being market day, by a fleet of portable stalls and open-sided trailers serving up the mouth-watering staples and treats beloved by locals and tourists alike.

Making his way past a stand of purple cabbages, Baldwin saw Tante Vivienne holding out a waffle folded in half, a delightful U-shaped valley filled with fresh strawberries and a dollop of cream. It was bulging from its wrap in a sheet of waxed paper. The sweet smell wafting from the window of the closely confined trailer was enough to make him want to devour several of them, but he confined himself, as always, to the complimentary one his aunt provided.

"You know I'll pay you one day for all these, Tante Viv," he promised.

"*Nee, nee,* no need," she threw back at him in her throaty Flemish dialect, waving her hand with a flutter, dismissing his offer with a warm smile only to turn to her next customer with an impassive look of expectancy. The mask of brief enjoyment had slipped.

Baldwin, he was called by his family at the insistence of his Oncle Marcel. His birth certificate read *Boudwijn* as arranged by his father. His baptismal certificate *Baudouin* after his mother's preference — both of which Oncle Marcel thought a backward continuation of the language tension forever plaguing the land.

Baldwin was athletic in build with slightly wide shoulders for his slim physique, a natural long-distance runner. His aunt often remarked on his golden-blond hair, which stood up with a swirl on his high forehead, the gift of a cowlick that defied taming. His deep-blue eyes had a calming, penetrating effect during direct conversations, that is, when he was confident enough to hold the other person's visage without looking away in a mix of self-consciousness and deference.

He had just turned eighteen and had been saving up for years as an apprentice to his uncle at the bustling dockyards nearby in Knokke-Heist. On occasion, he also did some odd jobs for his Oncle Etienne at the nearby mill, although he hadn't done much of that lately, which puzzled him, since he knew his boyhood pal Remi was getting requests.

Today though, he was particularly excited, having learned the day previous that Oncle Marcel had popped a bonus in his bank account, a long-promised sum of money held in trust for him by the uncle and aunt who had raised him after the death of his mother of a persistent pneumonia when he was only a toddler. He'd often wondered about his father, but it wasn't until he was nine or ten years old that he finally asked about the man he couldn't remember.

His Tante Viv had fielded the question. "Child, your father left for France to find work, and I'm afraid he never came back. We really don't know where he is. Perhaps he got ... scared of the responsibility of raising you, a young boy. He was a boy himself, just nineteen when you were born. But we just don't know…"

Not much of an explanation. Baldwin, expressionless, buried these painful thoughts, determined to find answers in due time. He started to wonder himself as he turned thirteen, seeing the love offered by his aunt and uncle, what could lead a man to make such a decision.

Waffle gone and fingers licked, he made his way past the market stalls to the Café Zonnebloem, where he knew his Oncle Marcel would be sitting with his older brother Etienne, enjoying their first of three or four *pintje* glasses of Jupiler together, out in the fresh air.

And there he was, Oncle Marcel, hulk-like, filling and spilling over a chair in his collared shirt, tightly pulled over a big barrel chest, gathered in with the aid of a pair of suspenders, *klocke* hat tilted at a jaunty angle, in need of a haircut as grey whisps protruded askew. His big bear-like hands were cupping the bottom of his dainty beer glass. Sometimes Baldwin wondered if one sneeze would shatter it, sending beer and glass astray. He was a kind man, given to largesse for his family, a generosity that extended to the upbringing of Baldwin following his sister-in-law's untimely death. His favourite role was to dress up as one of the bizarrely dressed giants during the numerous pageants put on in the villages and towns dotting the Flemish countryside in the midsummer festival months.

Oncle Etienne appeared much older than his brother and rather stork-like in visage and demeanour. His face was exceptionally slim, some would say pinched, and marked by very deep-set eyes, dark with a lingering shadow of the Spanish Netherlands period beneath a pair of bushy black eyebrows that seemed to blend into the flat cap that rarely left his head. Few but family and his postwar schoolmates would know of the protuberance of a wart that emerged above his left temple, forcing this same flat cap to be worn at a bizarre slope. No one ever questioned why. No one had the patience for a three-hour discussion with him on the proper cock of a hat. Suspicious by nature, Oncle Etienne was not improved by two other unfortunate habits. One was his steadfast adherence to chain-smoking his own rolled cigarettes, the other was his insistence on being right on any and every issue discussed since time immemorial. In truth, he was only six years older than Marcel, but throughout his long bachelorhood he'd set himself up as the self-proclaimed village sage, and on this day, his opinions would not be any different.

"Hey, young fella!" bellowed Marcel. "Her Indoors tells me you bought your tickets." His voice carried to the next block as if he was yelling to a stevedore at the end of the wharf. "She told me your plan. You don't do things by half do you? Constantinople no less!"

"Her Indoors" was his tongue-in-cheek reference to Tante Viv.

Baldwin had planned a long voyage since he was twelve years old, and confided in his aunt at sixteen. His own personal voyage, alone, according to his favourite book, to follow his namesake Baldwin, Count of Flanders, all the way to Constantinople in April of the year 1204 during what would become known as the Fourth Crusade. He poured over text after text and had long since moved past the holdings in the local Damme library. Monthly, he took buses into Bruges or Ghent to scour and absorb what was on offer regarding his favourite topic. He was continually frustrated in his inability to discover the final fate of the medieval Baldwin; it was not in any book or web page he had yet found. Though each harvest of knowledge culminated in a lively discussion with Oncle Etienne, often the following Sunday afternoon. A typical exchange looked like this…

"In France, they're sly, lazy and sit around drinking wine all day while the Flemish tend to their beets and carrots," Etienne would grumble.

"How do you know this, Oncle?" chimed Baldwin, baiting the hook.

"It's just a known fact. We've been sending them our *Fransmans* for hundreds of years."

"But I thought the *Fransmans* were hired workers. Does that make the French rich or lazy?"

"It makes them lazy, *Godverdomme*!!"

Or sometimes it might go like this…

"In Switzerland, they're all miserly bankers, squirrelling away all of the world's money," Etienne would puff out, quivering his thin lips, which he then rubbed rapidly with his nicotine-stained fingers to remove the small drop of spittle that marked the vehemence of his views.

"How do you know this, Oncle?" asked Baldwin, eager to hear about a land of gold and money.

"It's just a known fact. They all sit in their bank vaults, pale and ghostly like a horde of ghouls." He was getting heated.

"But I thought the Swiss also made some good-tasting chocolate and cheese?"

"That's only from the Flemish that moved there, idiot boy! *Godverdomme!!*"

And other times…

"In Italy, they're all lecherous, conniving crooks, ready to stab you with a dagger if you so much as cross their path or look at their sister the wrong way!" On this one, Etienne was extraordinarily convinced. "And they claim to have the nicest tomatoes! Let them compare with mine, where one tomato can feed a family of four!"

"How do you know about their lawlessness and tomatoes, Oncle?" Baldwin would say, with more than a hint of skepticism.

"It's just a known fact. They all hide in the hills like Carbonari, for hundreds of years, waiting for passers-by to rob, or force them to marry their bearded sister."

"But I thought Bruges and the Flemish School, the first with oil paintings, was the Florence of the north, so they must have some civilized folks down there—"

"That's only from the Flemish that moved there to teach them! *Godverdomme!!*"

These tirades proceeded in much the same way for the Germans, the Spanish, the Greeks and for all of Europe's peoples that did not reside in West Flanders, with particular venom reserved for the high-minded *kaaskop*, cheesehead Dutch — heathen protestants, snobbish usurpers of the Flemish talent, the likes of Pieter Bruegel, Vincent van Gogh and even Sint-Nicolaas … *Godverdomme!*

Baldwin got the feeling that in his gruff, awkward way, Oncle Etienne didn't want him to go on his long journey, perhaps being a bit jealous that he himself had never braved the endeavour, but also for other reasons, shadows of hints, often in whispers between his uncles that stopped suddenly when he entered a room.

The Sunday prior to his departure, Tante Vivienne had prepared a lunch of raisin bread, pistolets, ham, carpaccio, fine cheeses, pâtés, oliebollen and merveilleux for the family and close friends, all sprawled on a large table in the sitting area of their cottage garden. The invitation included Baldwin's schoolmate since childhood, Remi, his Liégeoise partner Yvonne and a few of the nearest neighbours. The mood was light, and all wished Baldwin a wonderful trip. Small gifts of money were plopped into his front shirt pocket with requests he raise a glass when he got to this city or that, memorable places visited here and there on past honeymoons and family vacations dotting the map of Europe. Baldwin laughed. He knew he could never hope to visit them all, but he was touched and felt deep appreciation, nonetheless, at the kind gestures.

After numerous goodbyes, and when most had left, Remi and Yvonne stayed behind for a final glass of beer and a heartfelt exchange. One of Tante Viv's cats, a black-and-white one she dubbed Phonse, jumped on Remi's lap to participate. Remi waved a well-chewed blue plastic toy that was once possibly Schtroumpf à Lunettes in front of Phonse, prompting a sudden bite to his thumb. Both the cat and his beer glass went flying as he jumped up in pain, a spot of blood appearing to justify his yelp. Remi's face had changed colour to match.

"*Godverdomme, strontzak kat!*" he yelled, sucking in air and shaking his hand vigorously.

He was prone to yelling and making a scene when things didn't go his way. Yvonne looked to Remi, her eyes wide, eyebrows raised and mouth tight. She hissed, "*Alors, Visloupe!* There you go, fish lips! Go inside and wash your hand. It was your fault, always having to tease every animal you play with. Make sure to use soap and wrap it in something until we get home."

He had gone inside before she finished her rebuke. She then listened for a moment, and without much warning, she grabbed Baldwin's hand and squeezed it. An exchange of rapid-fire whispers began.

"He's driving me nuts lately. It's worse now because he sees me distracted by something and then I can't get him to stop complaining about the smallest things. I know he works hard for the railroad, but ever since your Oncle Etienne asked him to help, his attitude has changed."

"*Mô*, let me guess, he's becoming more and more of a know-it-all?" Baldwin quipped.

"Yes, exactly! And ... I-I can't believe you're going already this week. I knew it was coming but ... it still feels so sudden..." she whispered sadly, running out of breath.

Baldwin had been out with Yvonne and Remi on numerous occasions over the past year. Remi had always had a wandering eye, which annoyed Baldwin, particularly since he immediately took to Yvonne as a bright person, full of life. Over beers in the café, Remi had bragged about his new girl from Liège only five minutes after he'd trashed the well-endowed girl from Oostende that he'd been seeing for eight months previous who had "put out." Baldwin didn't know if there was any overlap, but didn't care to ask. He had other matters on his mind. He had just broken off dating his childhood sweetheart, Sabine, at the time. Sabine had fallen in with the Bruges "it" crowd and cared more for appearances than character, which was a turn-off for Baldwin.

Sensing their limited time to talk, Baldwin turned to Yvonne and replied with resignation, "I know, but I need to go."

"But I'll be stuck here. I-I can't stay with Remi."

"I told you, I'm going for me — *and* for you. You need time. It's a big decision ... and I don't want to pressure you. I want you to think it through and, if it's meant to be, so be it ... and I think he needs to be honest with you too."

"Honest about what?"

"Well for one, about what he does when he's away from you. You've already noticed that he's out every Wednesday with my Oncle Etienne. Why does he have so many business trips with the railroad to Leipzig? I could see maybe Aachen, a transfer point, but Leipzig? It's in the former East Germany. And what does he do with the money he always seems to have? He takes you nowhere, and—"

"How do you know this?" She looked shocked and angry that he'd been holding back information.

"Look … Remi and I go way back but … we aren't friends like we used to be. Things have changed. And lately, it seems like something is going on, something that might affect both of us."

"What's going on? Baldwin, I—"

"I don't know. It's just a feeling." They were silent with their own thoughts for a few minutes until he turned to her again. "I'll text you if something big comes up, but please, think about what you really want." His voice carried a sort of low urgency, and he held her eyes for a long moment.

"All fixed!" Remi's booming voice startled them and they both turned toward him as he approached with a bemused look on his face and with a mound of gauze and a full roll of medical tape around his thumb, which was now as large as an Anjou pear. Despite the previous mood, and perhaps to cover it up, they all busted out laughing at the sight.

"What did you do?" asked Yvonne, grinning and pointing at the makeshift dressing that would embarrass an army field officer.

"Well, I ran into your Tante Viv, and I was dumb enough to explain what happened. She felt bad because it was her cat and kept me there for over twenty minutes wrapping this monstrosity around my thumb." He shook his head and smiled at the absurdity. "Yvonne, we should go. I've got to work tomorrow and I'm sure Baldwin has some things to take care of before he heads off this week."

"*Oui, bien sûr.* Yes, let's go."

To observe proper order, Baldwin gave Yvonne a kiss on each cheek and a brief hug and then exchanged with Remi an exaggerated man-hug, the one where each idiot squeezes the hardest to prove who's the man. Baldwin, slighter in build, gave in first. His face red, he tapped out and smacked Remi lightly with a quick right hand on the left cheek as Remi let him go.

"Safe travels, man!" Remi said. "And stay out of the brothels!"

"Don't worry, mate. I don't need to pay for it!"

"Okay," Yvonne said, shaking her head. "*Assez de conneries.* Enough foolishness, He-Man. We're off."

Two days before to his departure, Oncle Etienne took Baldwin aside as he was out walking Leopoldje. They walked slowly together along a narrow street in town, away from the café and out of earshot of the perpetually curious. "You look a lot like your father used to, you know. Blond as Jommeke, blue-eyed as a prince, a right spritely slim frame," muttered Etienne, as if each word begrudged him even more than the previous one.

"I do?" Baldwin had a sudden urge to step in front of a mirror. "In all these years, you've never really told me anything about him. Now that I'm heading off, I'd like to know."

Etienne grunted and turned away from his nephew.

"Oncle, please!" Etienne stopped, and Baldwin took this as a sign to continue. "What was my father like? Please, Oncle…" His earnest eyes were wide and bright, searching for the faintest of clues.

At this plea, a pained look came across the old man's face, almost as if a lingering lesion had come unstitched deep down in the recesses of his mind, and it now threatened to curtail this awkwardly frail effort at goodwill.

"Well, I really don't know how much I'm free to tell you, for family reasons you see…"

Again, the cryptic response. Hints of something more left unsaid, just out of reach. Baldwin looked over toward the windmill in the distance for a few moments, barely visible from the foot of the street. When he looked back, Etienne's face was shaking with a wave of palsy that sent the end of his most recent cigarette flying to the cobbles. He leaned against the stone frame of a small recessed chapel in the wall.

The expression on the face of the chipped and faded Virgin Mary figure mounted within seemed to match that of Baldwin, waiting in earnest for his response.

The spasm passed, and Etienne met his nephew's eyes. "I know your parents loved you … I used to see it in the way your father, my baby brother Erik, would look at you — and then at me with tears in his eyes, like he couldn't bear to think the thoughts he was thinking. Your mother noticed it too and it often led to a nasty squabble between the two of them, always away from you though, away from the rest of the family."

With this utterance, gruff, deep and guttural, he left off with a hacking cough that made it seem as though even this meagre admission would send him off to the *ziekenhuis* for a lengthy stay.

"Why, Oncle?" Baldwin asked, again hoping to finally winkle out a straight answer.

The spasm subsided once more, but a dark shadow still gripped Etienne's pinched visage as he spit out his last offering.

"One morning … your father up and left. I wasn't best pleased … but I thought you should know since you're heading away and insisting on visiting all those scoundrels from other countries I've been warning you about that will take your money, th-that money is … is…"

In an awkward gesture, he mussed up Baldwin's hair, shook his head, gave one last glance to the windmill and skulked away toward his cottage on the back lane behind Ons Lieve Vrouw Church.

Baldwin had left off listening, dwelling on the saddest part of what he'd just heard…

One morning, your father up and left…

He stooped down, hugged Leopoldje, scratching him behind his floppy ears, and set off for one last walk along the canal to get his thoughts straight.

The day had come. Baldwin had his train ticket and map in hand, old-school travel like he envisioned since he was twelve, and was ready for a proper Grand Tour that would take him gradually east and south through the Ardennes, through the scenic hills of the Vosges, over the Rhine, on to the Schwarzwald, to the Munich beer halls, through Vienna, Bratislava, Budapest and deep into the Balkans, with a stop at Sofia, all following the route of the renowned Orient Express to Istanbul. He hugged and waved goodbye to Oncle Marcel and Tante Vivienne at the station in Bruges. Oncle Etienne had refused to come, as if the courtesy of a final wave might be interpreted as an endorsement of a prodigal adventure. Yvonne did not appear either. Though he understood why, he still thought about it.

The train pulled out and he set off on his epic adventure, still pondering his uncle's explanation: *One morning, your father up and left…* He parked the thought, took a deep breath, popped a Leonidas praline chocolate in his mouth and sat back in his coach chair, ready to see the world.

Five months later, Baldwin's train pulled into Sofia's main station. Alighting in late July, he was immediately struck by the heat and exhilaration of being in his sixth new country since leaving home. Departing the station, he looked around and spotted the towering Vitosha mountain in the southwest, standing sentinel over the city that dated back at least seven thousand years and named after the Greek word for wisdom. Like Adrianople and Constantinople itself, a city at the crossroads of continents and empires.

He chuckled at the thought of Oncle Etienne trying to describe this ancient land of Thracians and Bulgars, with its Slavic language, a Cyrillic alphabet resembling a mix of Latin and Greek but robust and well entrenched for hundreds of years. He discovered with a vicarious pride for the country he was travelling through that the Russians had adopted the alphabet, the most ignorant of them thinking it was of their own making rather than the hard work of two dedicated Bulgarian monks, Saints Cyril and Methodius, and their followers. In general, he couldn't help but notice that his uncle's views proved to be a very skewed version of reality of the many peoples he'd visited en route;

views that were either out of date or outright inaccurate. It surprised him how a combination of second- and third-hand information together with belligerence had firmly cast his uncle in a self-satisfied state of ignorant contentment. As he thought about it, he realized that everyone needs to feel that they belong, and perhaps his uncle's authoritative manner of throwing opinions around was one of the only states of belonging he'd ever known. He smiled and thought of sending his uncle a postcard of himself sitting on the most expensive barstool in town, a borrowed drink for a prop and the caption "Wish you were here!! Their sports heroes are all Flemish! They call me Eddy Merckx!!" But he knew it would be disrespectfully mean and probably over the head of his uncle anyway.

With no clear agenda in Sofia other than to visit the famed Nevski Cathedral, he set off on a tram along Maria Louisa, past the Banya Bashi Mosque, and got off in a large central plaza in front of the domes of the lovely Sveta Nedelya Cathedral. Finding the heat and stuffy air on the tram unpleasant, he decided to walk, clinging to shadows as he made his way toward the President's Building. He was soon delighted to find himself in a charming outdoor market near the archaeological museum. He sat briefly on a bench under a plane tree and enjoyed the comings and goings of street buskers, chestnut vendors and an old heavy-set Romani woman sorting through a trash bin in the distance. A woman sitting on a low wall had dyed her hair an alarming carrot red. Carrot Head sat preening herself pensively while chatting on her mobile, cigarette in hand, evidently taking a break from her job at a nearby gift shop. Two other women walked by chatting together, one very animated, tall and rail thin with an infectious laugh, the other with striking blue eyes and delightfully curly hair. Lingering nearby was another woman with auburn hair, with two blond-haired boys making their way along with a rabbit's gait. The younger was stuttering his stroll to wipe his hands on his shorts as he licked the ice cream off the bottom of his cone, which he'd bitten off for reasons known only to himself. The scene was enhanced by an older gentleman playing the accordion on the walk leading to a monument to the Russian liberators of Bulgaria from the Turks in the 1870s.

Baldwin walked farther along, and the open square framed the Nevski Cathedral perfectly. With his small camera, a parting gift from Tante Viv, Baldwin hustled out onto the wide Moskovska Street to take a shot while traffic was at low ebb. In appreciation, he vowed that in lieu of waffle recompensation, he would gift her some photos from his trip, maybe framing a few later at home.

A more practical thought struck him. He took out his mobile phone and took a self-portrait with the cathedral behind him, chuckling after realizing he'd only managed to capture himself and the women and two boys he'd been watching earlier, who had innocently bombed his photo. *I guess this is God's way of helping me preserve the memory.* He smiled and then took another, his face beaming beside the graduated series of domes, then he dashed to the curb to avoid the onrush of the next wave of cars. He loved exploring. Nearby, a street vendor was selling what appeared to be a round pan of phyllo pastry.

"Apple? *Yabŭlka?*" Baldwin ventured, which dried up one of his vocabulary of seventy Bulgarian words. The vendor was a man in his forties with curly greying hair hanging in long waves around a round face that had a distinct dark mole on the left side of his chin.

"*Ne, ne ... Banitsa ... e dobre ... feta ... with cheese ... met kaas,*" replied the struggling polyglot.

Baldwin paid the man with the leva notes in his pocket and promptly bit into the delicious sweet pastry punctuated with salty feta cheese, a combination he would get to know and love in the coming weeks, along with an enormous variety of mouth-watering baked dishes — stuffed peppers, eggplant and the savoury meatball-like *kufteta*. He also learned to enjoy, both in bars and squirrelled away in the pantry cabinets of all self-respecting Bulgarian families, the potent brandy liqueur known as rakia. On finishing his snack, Baldwin again approached the vendor.

"*Molya?* Er … Please? *Da*, um, yes, is there a fortress here in Sofia? Castle?"

"Hmm … *né*, better you go Veliko Tarnovo. You have *karta*? A map?"

Baldwin reached into his rucksack with the small Belgian flag Tante Viv had embroidered on the flap and pulled out a map of Bulgaria he'd purchased at the station in Belgrade. He hadn't had time to study it before falling asleep on the train, his head a bit foggy from the *sljivovica* plum brandy he shared with a friendly middle-aged Slovene woman who took a shine to him. Once unfolded, the vendor poked at a city about two hours northeast. "*Tuka*, here," he offered as he stabbed his finger into the map. "Veliko Tarnovo … big castle … Tsarevets. You go, you like, *e dobre*." The man nodded, smiling.

"*Blagodaria* … uh … *Gospodin*. Thank you, sir." Baldwin fumbled through, using up two more of his Bulgarian words.

Vaguely recalling from his readings that Bulgaria had two periods as an empire, early with a khan, later during the Crusades with a tsar, Baldwin reassessed his plan to head straight to Istanbul. *It's not far off my route*, he mused, and then made his way back to the station to change his fare.

"*Dobre mi e!*" Baldwin sang. He was feeling good and getting into the local groove as he stretched and got off the coach in the blinding midday heat in front of the Veliko Tarnovo bus station. He went inside and ordered a café frappé to prepare himself to explore the capital of

Bulgaria's second empire. Refreshed, he wandered up a pleasantly shaded street, passed a military academy and came to a small plaza about halfway to the centre of town. The vista to the south confirmed the map's detail that the city hugged a huge meander in the river Yantra, some buildings dating back centuries, clinging to the terraced slopes in an enchanting mixed cityscape that delighted Baldwin, who was used to the flat polders of Flanders. Far below, he noticed a needle-like monument on the end of the first land point in the meander. It was framed beautifully by low mountains and seemed to beckon the sun to find the city's panorama of brightly coloured restaurants and café terraces.

Working his way up to the top of a T-junction, he reached ul Gurko, what appeared to be the oldest of the city's streets following the twisted Yantra. He found respite in one of three large marble drinking fountains set into the retaining wall of the slope above, dotted with older apartments and hotels offering alternatively lovely views of the valley or partly shaded backstreets. As he stood up again, a blond boy, one of the two travelling with their mother he'd noticed in Sofia, nearly smacked him in the jaw with an errant yo-yo before his mother intervened, entreating him to be more careful with his weaponry. Baldwin shook his head and wondered, *Is it a coincidence to see the same kids?*

On ul Gurko, he wandered in and out of newer shops that carried a vast collection of modern sporting apparel, shoes of all makes and sizes, designer watches and handcrafted costume jewellery. He wanted to send something to Tante Vivienne, something unique and not found on the high street of any large town across northwestern Europe. As he moved eastward, following the rim of the gorge below, the shops became more touristy, with the typical assortment of beloved tack: spoons and tea towels, bottle openers and refrigerator magnets, folksy handicrafts and the ubiquitous pottery plates with a drab brown sketch of the local cathedral. Coming out of one shop, he lingered in the doorway to take advantage of the blasting air conditioner and noticed three small striped tabby cats languidly stretched out on the low walls around an empty bowl and one jet-black kitty curled up in the shade of a small lemon tree that adorned the sidewalk in a low planter.

The tourist kitsch blended into a stretch of smaller shops of curios and antiques. More stalls than stores, some of them could cope with no more than one or two visitors at a time exploring the mix of wares stacked from floor to ceiling. Steamer trunks and small hall tables, cigarette cases and lighters, toy soldiers, pocket watches, swords, daggers, pistols and army helmets — Bulgarian, Russian and Nazi military caps from the Second World War and Cold War eras, swastikas competing with the hammer and sickle for prominence in viewing space, as if the competition for hearts and minds continued into the new millennium.

Knowing his aunt's passion for lace, Baldwin found a shop displaying a rich assortment of Bulgarian millinery and linens, many adorned with intricate lace and capturing classic Bulgarian runes, Cyrillic characters and the folkloric moustachioed men in leather vests, fiddling or dancing in a circle, holding hands with busty maidens modestly covering their dark locks in scarves. He picked out an embroidered lace-fringed scarf with a large letter B adorning one corner. He could already foresee the confusion reigning in the Damme *markt* as the treasure was displayed by his Tante Viv. *Why a B? Silly boy. My name starts with V!*

Baldwin knew from experience that his bizarre sense of humour wasn't always shared, but on this day he didn't care. He wanted to see how many at home would make the link to another alphabet, where the B is pronounced as a V, an amusement saved for his eventual return home. He had it packaged by an elderly woman with jet-black eyes framed in rimless spectacles, with thin lines for eyebrows and grey hair pulled up into an enormous bun. Her dress was ornate, her movements slow and purposeful, her manners easy and gestures smooth, hinting at a once gentrified life for a woman whose needs in her later years had pushed her to take on a new role as shopkeeper and grand dame of one of the finer boutiques on the street. Baldwin tucked away his package, thanking her with "*blagodaria*" and a nod, exercising twice in two days his new found vocabulary for appreciation.

Snacking on some almonds he found in his pack, he came finally to the lure prompting the detour in his itinerary, the gates of the Tsarevets Fortress. He paid his entry fee and stopped at the soft-drink vendor where the thermometer read 42°C. A weathered man of about his height, whose mannerisms were somehow familiar, sold him a bottle of water and stared at the miniature Belgian flag Tante Viv had embroidered on his small rucksack. Baldwin downed the water, then, refreshed to some degree, walked up and stopped in front of a large stone pillar, a regal looking lion atop, marking the beginning of a flagstone causeway that formed the only entry to the indomitable fortress set within the largest loop of the Yantra. Steep slopes formed a daunting, naturally protective barrier on all other sides, guarding the walled enclosure with a remarkable array of defences from prospective medieval invasion.

Within the entrance to the walled enclosure, past the intimidating portico gate, was a bizarre diorama of puppetry, curious novelties that included squirting water and mechanical gestures, as if the cast of *The Little Drummer Boy* were given a renewed life in the tsar's place of honour.

Baldwin climbed the long stone walk to the small basilica at the top of the highest point, marvelling at the more modern painting and iconography contained within the structure. Outside, there were wonderful vistas in all directions, the full meander of the river gorge coming into view, marking for Baldwin the wisdom of this choice of location for an impregnable fortress. On the north slope, a large flag of Bulgaria marked the buildings of the royal palace. In the southwest, a modest fifty-foot square tower with crenulated roof battlements set watch over the southern exposure of the roughly hewn but regal complex. Baldwin checked the small map he'd received on entry, noting with some delight that the tower held the moniker "Baldwin's Tower."

"Baldwin's Tower, how much of a coincidence is that?" he said aloud, in wonder.

"Perhaps not much of a coincidence…"

Baldwin spun around to see the weathered man from the soft-drink stand sitting on the wall in the shadow of an umbrella pine, his small cart of cold drinks parked beside the intersection of two sun-baked stone walkways. Baldwin looked more closely at him this time. The man wore a plain blue T-shirt with casual brown pants over a slim frame. His only treat to himself looked to be a pair of well-worn but high-quality Italian leather shoes.

"You're Belgian, no?" the man asked.

"Are you following me?" Baldwin blurted.

"*Mô*, perhaps it is you who are following me, but we shall see," the man retorted in Flemish Dutch.

Baldwin gawked at the man, shaking his head, muttering, "*Nee, nee*" as if in protest to a false accusation, but astonished to hear so clearly the home dialect of his mother tongue.

The man whistled to a bearded companion on the far side of the small clearing, asking him in a series of demonstrative gestures to watch his cart for him.

He turned to Baldwin. "Walk with me, please?" He gestured to the walkway along to the tower.

Baldwin hesitated, but when the man turned, he followed him to the path from the basilica. Together they walked past a hedgerow of fragrant boxwood to a viewpoint just upslope of the tower that had been highlighted in the entrance brochure.

The man stopped suddenly and turned to Baldwin. "Why did you come here?"

Somewhat surprised and annoyed at the tone of the question, Baldwin replied, "I've always wanted to travel. This fortress was recommended to me in Sofia and happened to be near enough on my route."

"But you know this place?" the man persisted.

"I only know it in a sense that it was recommended, as I said. I'm on my way to Constantinople … Istanbul," Baldwin admitted, wondering where this strange conversation with this strange man was going.

The man studied his face for an uncomfortable few minutes, then said, "Constantinople … Istanbul … why?"

Baldwin had been travelling for close to six months. He had explored the Alsatian vineyards of the Vosges, enjoyed the festive beer gardens of Munich, the Hapsburg splendour of Vienna, the spicy Magyar cuisine in Budapest and the rugged zest for life of Belgrade, but no one had asked him why he'd ventured from his home in Flanders, and to this point, it didn't seem to matter to anyone but himself, the way he liked it.

"Well ... it's been my goal since childhood." Baldwin was opening up. He didn't know why. This man was a stranger but there was a strange connection occurring. He couldn't give it a label yet.

As if their thoughts were shared, the man asked, "Do you know the connection between this tower and Flanders?"

"*Nee, nee,*" Baldwin admitted, shaking his head, confounded.

The man began to walk again, motioning him to follow. Approaching the tower, he mounted the small ledge leading up to a stone stairwell wrapped around the northern edge of the tower, with an open entrance to a pleasantly shaded bare room within. They leaned against the wall and rested momentarily.

"In this tower," the man said, "Baldwin the First, one of the most famous of the Flemish counts, was imprisoned. That's why it still holds the name Baldwin's Tower. The crusader died here in 1205."

Baldwin shook his head. "That's not true. Baldwin led the Fourth Crusade conquering the Byzantines and became the first Latin Emperor of the Eastern Empire as Baldwin the First of Constantinople. Why would he die *here*?"

"After taking Constantinople, he was later captured by the Bulgarians during the Battle of Adrianople. A sad way to go in the end for a medieval noble."

Still stone-faced, the man pressed further. "This history interests you?"

"*Ja,* well. I've read about it since I was a young boy."

"And where did you get your information? School?"

"*Ja,* some ... but most from one of my favourite books, a text left in my family home in Damme."

On hearing this, the man's face transformed from a smug expression of grade-school pedantry to one that seemed to tap into a long-buried painful emotion and then finally to a mix of hope and cautious curiosity. In one last effort, to be absolutely sure of himself, or more likely to ensure the avoidance of disappointment, he lobbed out one last query.

"Perhaps because 1205 was when he died, past the book's date range, but never mind that…" He was muttering this and buying time while searched for the right words. "You mention Damme, a town of which I have some knowledge. Did you perhaps have as your bedside companion a text entitled *The Crusades 1000–1200* as the source of your inspiration on Baldwin the Count?"

This hit Baldwin like a brick. He could barely nod he was in such a state of disbelief.

The man absorbed this for a few moments, then tilted his head as he said, "You're called Boudwijn?"

"*Ja* … well, Baldwin … but h-how do you know?"

"Are you now around eighteen? You have an uncle … Marcel? Tante Vivienne?"

"*Ja* … *M-mô* … how? *Varoom?* Why…?"

Silence. The words the man wanted to say should have been simple, but they were difficult to craft in a way that would make up for the years of pain and uncertainty. "Boudwijn — sorry, Baldwin, I believe … I believe strongly that I'm your father … my name is Erik."

This was too much. Baldwin became dizzy and confused, his throat parched from the heat, the new information too much to be digested, and his brain spiralled in a daze. He stared at the man … Erik … in disbelief.

"Come with me, please," Erik pleaded, and it didn't take much to coax Baldwin away from the intense heat near the tower to a nearby walnut tree where he could sit on a low wall and collect his wits away from the sunlight. Erik offered him another bottle of water from his bag, and then the two men walked together in silence. Baldwin was too stunned to object. He followed Erik from the complex to a shady table in a café. The only other patron was an older man with a kind face, reading a newspaper, sipping on a Kamenitza pilsner.

"You … you're my father?" Baldwin finally mustered. "Why now? Why here? You … you went to France."

"I worked there for two years, sending money back to your mother. One day I received a note from your Oncle Etienne that your mother had died. I never knew whether she'd ever received the money

I sent, as your uncle controlled the family finances. He also told me that I should feel ashamed for taking fifteen thousand francs — it was francs back then — which he felt belonged to him."

"But … what? You took fifteen thousand francs?"

"*Nee*, I put fifteen thousand francs, money I'd earned at the windmill working for your uncle, in the bank as a trust fund for you when you turned of age. This I mentioned to your Oncle Marcel, and I have the pay slips to prove it. By what turned out to be coincidence, fifteen thousand francs went missing from the safe in the mill office that Etienne kept on hand for reinvestment or for maintenance, depending on the needs for the coming work year. I didn't take it, but the sums were the same, so he figured I'd taken it."

"But you had proof … your pay slips."

"Son — if you'll allow me to call you that, as I have much to make up to you — when I was your age I was … wayward, unsettled. The family put little faith in me to accomplish anything of importance. My marriage to your mother at nineteen, bless her, was arranged within days of knowing that you were going to come into the world. She was sweet but sickly and not much better than I was at keeping a level head and planning our future. So when it came down to my word against my older brother Etienne's, there was no way anyone would support me. I felt horrible about this stain on the family, and I couldn't bear to have that legacy fall on your shoulders, so I took off, and I feel daily the most intense shame imaginable for abandoning you to your aunt and uncles."

Absorbing this, it was Baldwin's turn to press.

"So you went from France to … Bulgaria?"

"*Nee*, not directly." He chuckled and stopped very quickly, as if catching himself in a sick joke.

"I'd send postcards out of spite to your Oncle Etienne from all the places I stopped to work. From France telling him the people were lazy and drank wine all day, from Italy that all were thieves with daggers and ugly bearded women, from Switzerland that all Swiss were ghouls haunting bank vaults. I don't know what he ever made of them or who he told about them, but it was my small way of poking him in the eyes and feeding his bigotry to make him look ridiculous."

For the first time since this onslaught of information hit him, Baldwin smiled. "Well, it worked … we can talk about this later … but first … why are you here in Bulgaria?"

"My goal since childhood…" Erik sighed. "I travelled to Istanbul and back here to follow the medieval Baldwin's life. Do you think you were the first to read that text by your bedside?"

Baldwin absorbed this with a bemused smile and then raised his eyebrows and cocked his head to pose a question, looking to remain polite. "But … a cart vendor?"

Erik laughed. "Yes, living the dream!" He then lowered his voice and looked around, saying quietly, "I'll explain all in due time."

They chatted animatedly for three hours, after which the kindly newspaper reader was joined by a woman and two boys, one with a yo-yo. The man was giving the smaller of the two boys a stuffed red-and-gold monkey. Baldwin saw them, smiled at the recurring coincidence and was filled with inward bliss. He had been released from the burden of not knowing a mystery that had lingered with him his whole life, and he still had plenty to discuss with the man he could now call Father.

PART 2

BELIEF

Together, Baldwin and Erik travelled southwest from Veliko Tarnovo, and they explored the renowned monastery of Rila. They marvelled at the detail of the bold yet spiritual basilica. Its impressively detailed frescoes and icons enlivened the cool dark interior and seemed all the more holy with the flickering light of the massive arrangements of votive candles. The exterior was even more alive with colourful scenes and stark murals depicting the fates of those living a moral life versus the damnation and trials of those slipping toward devilry and evil. Despite warning signs not to do so, Baldwin took photos surreptitiously, mostly of his favourite subject, old doors. In one, he was pleased to capture a tall austere bearded figure in black robes, the monk on duty that day, making the monastery and the Lord's calling his home.

As they exited through the back, Baldwin took photos of faces, pilgrims and other visitors in the silhouette made by the corridor of the rear gate. In the shade of a pine near a chestnut stand, Erik and Baldwin took a break to sip water and watch the souvenir vendors.

"So tell me a little of Damme. Marcel and Viv are good?"

Baldwin nodded. "Yeah, Oncle Marcel is slowly getting bigger, but he still gets around, driving people nuts with his jokes. He still makes me laugh, but I see people rolling their eyes at some of them that are just so bad. Tante Viv though … I think she's getting tired of the waffle stand, getting up very early prepping every day. I noticed she's pretty tired at night. She doesn't do too much except talk to her cats. We have a dog, Leopoldje, who chases the cats around now and then. I think he enjoys bugging the crap out of her because he still wags his tail when she yells at him."

Erik laughed. "And the town — still drawing day-trippers from Bruges?"

Baldwin shrugged. "Damme is fine. They've been adding houses for years, but I don't think the *markt* and centre have changed much. Still lots of tourists and getting busy along the canal tow path. Some say now there's way too many people."

"And who are your friends? I recall a young boy about your age living two doors down—"

"Remi! Yeah, he's still around."

"And he's a runner like you? Wandering about with a backpack?"

"Remi? He'll never leave Damme. The only place Remi likes to go is the Red Light District in Amsterdam or I guess sometimes the dockyard."

Baldwin didn't elaborate and say that he could barely get Remi off the couch most days. Remi preferred to spend his evening watching sports with a beer when he wasn't working for the railway. He'd gained a lot of weight in the past few years, and Baldwin smirked as he thought of his friend trying to ride a bike. This led to a slight but doleful smile, as he knew this was a lame way to think of his friend, although their friendship seemed to be in an awkward state of flux. They hadn't really been what he would call close friends for some time, given how Remi was treating Yvonne.

Erik noticed Baldwin's face fade into a distant look, as though something were preoccupying his thoughts. He didn't press, but took note. Both father and son were still slowly and respectfully peeling back the layers on how much they would communicate.

Months later, they sat on a rooftop terrace in Istanbul overlooking the Bosphorus under a hazy sky to the north and Gülhane Park down below to the east in the Eminönü quarter of the Old City.

"Maybe I shouldn't have come here to Istanbul with you," Erik muttered pensively under his breath while tapping the shell of an egg he'd reserved to the end of his breakfast. He'd already enjoyed some *beyaz peynir*, fresh cheese, olives, yogourt and freshly cut melon.

Baldwin looked up at him. "No…" As a young man who spent his childhood managing his expectations, he was still getting used to the unfamiliar exhilaration of having a father in his life, and he struggled to express his new feelings. With each perceived thought, each word, each action of his father, Baldwin felt like he never knew when fate or some higher power that presented his father might snatch him away. His words arriving, he blurted them out. "I know I'm still full of questions, which must … er … maybe … drive you nuts, but I'm glad you're here, and not just to show me around… I'm … I'm really glad you're here."

Erik smiled warmly, looked at his son, and replied, "I'll do my best with your questions. You deserve answers and I know there's still lots to discuss." He looked up pensively at the hazy sky over the harbour, and then seemed momentarily distracted by laughter from a neighbouring table. Then, realizing he'd left Baldwin hanging, looked him in the eyes and said, "And I'm glad you're glad. Me too."

It was their third day in the city. Both knew that prior to being conquered by the Turks in 1453, it was the celebrated city of Constantinople, for more than a thousand years the capital of the Byzantine Empire.

They'd spent the morning before on a cruise boat launched from the docks within sight of the Yeni Mosque and in the shadow of the Galata Bridge. A wonderful two-hour visual panorama, providing Baldwin with his first real glimpse of the decadent splendour stamped on the city by the Ottoman sultans. The cruise boat had inched eastward, where they parted the bridal veil of fishing lines dangling from both sides of the bridge, skirted beneath the roadway above and exited the sheltered natural confines of the Golden Horn into a wide open waterway. Baldwin recalled from his books and maps that they'd entered the outer harbour area where the Sea of Marmara meets the Bosphorus, the short narrow strait that forms a boundary between Europe and Asia, and which, along

with the Dardanelles downstream, connects the Black Sea ports to the
world through the Aegean and the Mediterranean.

Baldwin and his father had experienced a few adventures already
in their brief time together in Turkey. At the border entry near Edirne,
the passport control officials grilled Erik for forty minutes about why
he was returning to the country. As Baldwin watched, it was not easy
for him to explain in stilted English that he was returning as a tourist
with his son after having applied for a work visa five years ago. Baldwin
knew it would be of little use to try to explain that he'd just met his
father in Bulgaria after eighteen years of not knowing him! A middle-
aged man in uniform had taken Erik into a back room for further
questioning. Baldwin waited a half hour before another officious
looking man in a crisp suit and closely trimmed moustache entered the
back room and left within two minutes. Erik reappeared with the
uniformed security agent who looked sheepish and withdrawn, after
evidently having been given a terse dressing down by someone more
than three levels above his pay grade. On later questioning, Erik offered
little to Baldwin by way of explanation, noting dismissively that it may
have been a case of mistaken identity.

Once through Eastern Thrace and into Istanbul, their train had
snaked its way to its terminus at Sirkeci Station in the old quarter of the

city. As they walked out of the crowded station, a middle-aged Azeri man in a white shirt and brown slacks bumped into Erik roughly as he made his way through the crowd. They looked at each other as if in recognition, the man's eyes in earnest, Erik surreptitiously shaking his head as if to say, *Not now!* The man quickly nodded and disappeared behind a column, ignoring the small pile of change he had at his feet, accumulated by a Romani child sitting akimbo playing a battered recorder. East of the station, they found a budget hotel and rested briefly, intent on later that day exploring the wondrous city that Baldwin had read about in his youth.

Their dialogue as father and son had become deeper and more meaningful each day since their reunion two months ago in the middle of Bulgaria. *In the middle of Bulgaria of all places after eighteen years!* Baldwin thought. They'd decided to travel together to explore more of the region, Baldwin eager to learn more about this kind but reserved man he'd heard so little about since his childhood, Erik ready to fully embrace his long-neglected role as father to this remarkable young man he'd abandoned in his youth. Their travels eventually brought them to Istanbul.

"I'm still amazed at how many layers there are to this city. Each time I think I understand a little more, something new pops up. I'm already getting overloaded trying to keep matters straight between Byzantine, Latin, Greek, Ottoman, Genoese, Atatürk ... it will take me weeks to absorb it all."

Erik smiled a rueful smile. "I'm glad you still feel that way. Those men meant business at the border. You're lucky you read ahead to see what you needed. It was different when I was here five years ago; seems much more intense."

Slightly confused on the latter point, Baldwin refused to let it get him down. "It's everything that's been happening in the region these last few years, I guess — protests, bombings. No wonder they're so uptight at the borders. I didn't notice it anywhere else though; they were pretty relaxed on the boat tour yesterday."

"Yes, they were. I noticed the guide was a little over the top with the cost of all the palaces, and his crazy fixation on the sultans' harems was interesting. I thought that young German lady was ready to slug him." Erik chuckled.

Baldwin reached for his small coffee cup and finally voiced a niggling thought. "That guy at the station, what do you think he wanted? He looked like he knew you. Have you ever seen him before?"

Erik looked at him, then looked away dismissively, saying nothing. Baldwin watched him closely but didn't want to intrude too quickly into his father's life. It was quite evident it was not skepticism he felt though, but a new level of caring for this man who walked into his life only a short time ago.

As Baldwin took a sip of the coffee in his cup, he winced. "This coffee is strong. Look at the grinds in the bottom of my cup. Don't they filter it?"

Erik busted out into a teasing grin.

"So you've not heard of Turkish coffee then? That's their style: thick enough to stand up your spoon and bitter enough to keep you awake for hours. Anyway, we have more of this city to explore before we move on. Ready?"

"Yes, I have my Istanbul map! Let's go!" he replied eagerly.

They leaned over the terrace railing and took a photo of a man with an enormous belly chain-smoking down below at street level in front of his fruit stand, and then headed down to visit to the sultan's covered market.

The Grand Bazaar was nested in a whole block in the old quarter of the city, just west of the Topkapi Palace. Along the short walk toward its gate, they each picked up a glass of the fresh-squeezed orange juice that had become their favourite refresher and passed another older building with a sign Baldwin couldn't understand: *Cemberlitas Hamami*. Erik provided the translation when he saw Baldwin trying to make out the wording. "It's the Turkish bath the Sultan Mehmet built in the late fourteen hundreds, after conquering the city."

"It's still open? Who goes there?" Baldwin asked, puzzled that such an ancient structure would still be clean enough to bathe in.

"Many people, even tourists. This one will take you back in time if you enter. The marble is exquisite."

"But aren't public baths just meant for sweaty homeless old men?"

"*Nee, nee*, the Turkish bath is quite popular for all in their culture. Of course, they have separate baths for men and women. I had one once, it was quite something."

As they walked toward the bazaar, Erik described in detail and wonderment his bath experience during his last visit. He told Baldwin that, after paying a fairly modest fee at the entrance, he'd been ushered inward with a grunt and a hand signal by the bearded cashier's assistant to doff his clothes in a small room, and then, naked as his birthday, to don a small towel around his waist. He recalled wondering if the towel, coarse and rough and worn through in places, might date back to the late 1400s as well. Shuddering at the thought, he was then instructed by hand signal through a small corridor. The slim attendant directing him, wizened and dressed in a drab plum-coloured robe, must have seen his share of the ugliness of humanity inside the baths.

"He showed me through a huge doorway into something like a cavern filled with steam — well it was as large as one and with a domed ceiling. And it was so warm inside," Erik said as they continued their walk. "At first I thought I'd just sit in a quiet corner to watch what went on, but of course, there were no corners!" He went on to describe how an enormous man had appeared through the fog. "He pointed to a circular slab of marble in the centre, big enough for lots of people, I'd say spanning some six metres across," Erik said. "I didn't have much choice. So I sat."

Baldwin imagined how self-conscious he would feel in that situation. "Wow! I think I would have shit myself!"

Erik nodded. "Well, yes. I barely turned my head, but I wanted to see everything, so I just moved really slowly."

For the next ten minutes, he told Baldwin about the contrasting faces, shapes and sizes of the others present in the room in their own medieval loincloths; about the ornately carved marbled interior, the strategically placed windows to bring in sufficient but subtle light, the open cisterns of water along the room's periphery, the rising mist, ebbing and flowing as the two, sometimes three, attendants went about their work; and about the incredible warmth of the marble slab as he reclined, bringing out a sweat at a rate he'd not remembered since digging a ditch near a Rhone valley vineyard in the August heat. He described two others who joined him on the slab. One was a lacquered American who sat down briefly, decided it was too much of a challenge to his clean-cut Bible Belt ways and left through the exit hallway. The other was a tall slender fellow, ghostly pale with freckled skin, a hawk-like face and long red hair in a ponytail. He had an animated, friendly look, modestly clinging to his tiny towel as he offered in a fine Scottish brogue: "You looook rather waaarm, chief!"

Baldwin shared a laugh with his father. "The acquaintance was short lived though," Erik continued. Then he explained that the enormous man had reappeared and stood over him, staring for a few moments, giving Erik a chance to examine him more closely. He was covered in a pelt of hair stretching the boundaries of the definition of hirsute. Two metres tall, his shoulders were ripped and powerful, his neck somehow disappeared and reappeared as needed, and his presence coming through the mist in this chamber was announced first by an enormous belly protruding well in front over abusively stretched white briefs. His stone face looked as if it would hold the same expression regardless of whether he was slaughtering a goat or cuddling a child. Poker would have been a breeze. Then he whacked Erik's right foot and gestured him to follow him away from the slab and to lie down on the marble floor near the cistern, with only a small block of wood for a pillow.

Erik had barely settled when the man threw a large pail of water in his face and drained the rest along the length of his body. Still sputtering from this, the process was repeated, leading Erik to wonder if the Yank had got it right after all. Wiping the water from his eyes, he watched with lingering concern as the man then grabbed a burlap sack from a hidden compartment. The bag was dipped into another container and filled with a generous volume of soap suds, which were then dumped without apology in his face and over the length of his body. Looking down, he noticed with some alarm his nether bits exposed to all in the room and covered in suds. He rapidly twisted his towel to cover up what he certainly didn't want to advertise.

Sauntering away into the fog as if to let soak, The Belly soon came back, this time wearing a massive loofah glove, and grabbed first one arm then the other, then each leg, scraping like a painter on an old windowsill. At first alarmed at the vigour the man was putting into this, Erik watched in a sort of daze as a disgusting film of grey froth came off his skin, which, even in the dim light and mists of the room, now seemed to glow beneath the remaining suds in a painful red rage. Feet, neck, hands, armpits and perhaps a little too much time in the crotch, the skin on no part of the body was spared from this grating glove of searing redemption. The exercise was then punctuated by another waterboarding episode to cleanse away what the body didn't want to deal with anymore.

Clean from the rinse cycle, Erik thought that he must be nearing completion. "Not the case!" he told Baldwin. The Belly returned and again whacked his right foot, then made a roll-over gesture. "I really didn't know what was coming next," Erik confided, and told his son that he turned over with great reluctance, put his forehead on the shallow wooden pillow and expected the worst. To his surprise, the next session was a massage. Not in any dainty sense though. "That monster of a man kicked off his leather sandals and started walking on my back!" Erik described the unimaginable weight pressing down on his shoulders and how his generous Flemish nose started to crunch into the marble below, prompting a quick turn of his head to relieve the stress and to catch a glimpse of the medieval inquisitor doing a number on his back. After four or five minutes of agony and another waterboarding, he was dismissed with a grunt and a whack on the foot. The Scotsman had watched the whole thing, first in amusement, and then in wide-eyed disbelief.

Baldwin looked agog. "He really walked on your back!"

"You should have seen the bruises. I went to take a shower at the hostel and a man asked me, 'What the hell happened to you?' because he could clearly see footprints on my back, the veins spidering out from the hoof prints of that monster, as clear as a roadmap."

At this comment, Baldwin and Erik both burst into laughter as they approached the gates of the bazaar.

"I'm telling you, one forty would be fair," Baldwin barked at the vendor. "It's not worth much more. I looked around."

"But, my friend! This watch is not cheap imitation. Patek Phillipe. Look, you can turn it over and see the mechanism inside! Geneve. Swiss. Good. You like? I give you for two ten, yes?" The man was just getting warmed up.

"I'll come up to one sixty, but that's it. I don't need a watch that badly," Baldwin said, staring the man in his dark-brown eyes. He had a skin tag on his eyelid that fluttered up and down as he blinked.

Actually, Baldwin did covet a nice watch and saw it as an opportunity to gift himself with something memorable from his adventure that wasn't a tacky trinket.

"I give you for one eighty-five, okay?" the slim man smartly dressed in an embroidered shirt, slacks and sandals persisted, holding up the number on a battered calculator with enormous buttons and an even larger number display.

"One sixty-five. Last offer. Or I walk." Unconsciously, he'd slipped into the staccato of basic English in sympathy with the jewellery merchant.

With a pained expression, as if his eldest child had been denied a university education over the results of this sale, the man shook his head, repeating, "Swiss, Swiss!"

A few feet away, Erik was listening to this exchange between Baldwin and the vendor — until he was approached by a veiled woman who slipped him a mobile phone and then disappeared into the crowd. Erik looked down at the phone, pressed a button and then dashed over to join Baldwin. He stepped between Baldwin and the vendor, flipped open a bill-fold, counted out one ninety, handed it to the merchant and grabbed the watch.

"But—" Baldwin began to protest, a little annoyed that his father had stepped in and paid more than he wanted to.

"Let's go. We have to leave. Now." Erik put a strong hand on Baldwin's arm and moved him toward the nearest exit, north toward the spice market, leaving the merchant in puzzled disbelief, yelling down the corridor over a boy spinning a top, "*Monsieur!* You want in box?"

Rushing past the entrance, Erik noticed two blond boys and their mother sitting on stools in the slim passage, biting into doner kebabs. He stood behind them, beckoning Baldwin to do the same, and turned away as if to order an iced tea from the vendor. From the corner of his eye, Baldwin noticed two security patrolmen, *Polis* marked clearly on their black uniforms, rush into the market. Once they passed, Erik pulled Baldwin away to a small courtyard with a well in the middle and public toilets in the far corner. They stood in the shade of a back corridor to another street, where they could watch anyone approaching.

"What was that all about?" Baldwin demanded. "Are you on the run from the police?"

"I can explain, just not here, not now."

In the street, they heard a siren and more security arriving. After a few minutes, a young couple — he in dreadlocks with a beaded satchel, she a waif with a pierced lip, both dark in complexion — were dragged away from the market and into a police panel van. The van left, sirens stopped and the everyday bargaining and sipping of apple tea resumed as if it were still the year 1500.

After the excitement of the market, they went for a walk in Gülhane Park. The plane trees and chestnuts reminded Baldwin of his brief stay in Melnik in southern Bulgaria near the Greek border. Walking slowly with his father, who also seemed preoccupied and occasionally looked over his shoulder, Baldwin drifted into reverie.

Melnik was one of his favourite places from his brief travels through Europe. He was happy to discover the small town tucked away in Bulgaria's wine region, off the beaten track from the smug arrogance and trendiness of the tour-bus and backpacker circuit. He recalled his hotel experience there as one he would treasure forever, with the unexpected joy of tasting wines in a candlelit vintner's cave, and with dawn views of the timeless village nestled within steep sandstone valley walls carved by the elements into towers, bulging pinnacles and obelisks. He remembered the the delicious meals of yogourt, baked peppers, savoury stews and even quail eggs, a first for him, washed down with the rich red wines of the region. He recalled a short but challenging hike to the top of the valley to a tiny monastery, the scent of the pines, and the happiness he felt as he enjoyed the panoramic views. Nettles and thistles in the undergrowth had scratched his legs at the time, and now a small fly tickling his ankle brought him back to Gülhane Park.

His father also pulled him back to the present by pointing at a vacant park bench, a shady break from their long walk in the intense heat. "Sit, we must talk."

Baldwin was happy to get off his feet, but he couldn't quite relax. There were too many unanswered questions. "Are you going to tell me what that was all about? And who was that lady?"

"You noticed her?"

He nodded.

"She's ... an acquaintance. A coworker in a way."

"And that man in the train station?"

"Also an acquaintance."

"You work here?"

"Yes, but not in a conventional sense. It's a bit complicated."

"Try me, I have lots of time. Eighteen years to catch up."

This made Erik smile, his feelings for his son growing more deeply with each passing day.

"I'm what you might call a freelancer in the area of antiquities."

"What does that mean?"

"It means people rely on my expertise and knowledge for ancient artifacts, things like coins, pottery, jewellery."

"So you travel around? Why did you have that cart in Bulgaria? Do you have a base somewhere for your business?"

"I was on a short assignment in Bulgaria."

Baldwin was now thoroughly confused, having heard his father mention a Turkish work visa at the border and then seeing the strange Azeri at the station and the woman with the mobile phone in the market and now more facts that still did not all hang together. He wanted to believe in his father, but he also didn't know where this was going and it sounded loose and a bit shady.

"What types of assignments do you take on?"

Erik had wanted to keep things private for the safety of his son, but now realized that honesty was going to be necessary to ensure that his son trusted him, something he refused to let slip ever again.

"Are you familiar with antiquities, artifacts, precious objects and how they're bought and sold?"

"Well ... I'll have to admit, not really. I've read how some museums got things and that a lot of it was stolen from other countries hundreds of years ago—"

"I'm not talking about precious items stuffed in Western museums that were pilfered through colonialism back in the nineteenth century," Erik burst in. "I'm speaking of small items recovered today, through theft, illicit dealings, bribes, kickbacks, what have you. You're aware how this goes on?"

"No, not really..."

"Well, this region is loaded with archaeological finds and it's had its share of instability over the centuries and even more recently. That makes it easier to move precious items out of the country. Things go missing during upheavals."

"So how do you fit in?"

Erik took a sip from his water bottle and stared into Baldwin's eyes. "When I arrived here five years ago, I did something very foolish."

Baldwin waited, his pause hoping to draw his father out.

"I was travelling through Bulgaria where I met a man in Varna who asked me to deliver a package to his colleague in Istanbul. Thinking I was no drug mule, I declined. He then offered me five thousand leva to do this for him and assured me that drugs were not involved. I was very stretched for cash at the time, so I … I agreed."

"You got caught at the border?"

"No, I made it through the border, but when I arrived in Istanbul, I was intercepted by the MIT, the Turkish Secret Police. They opened the package. It contained Thracian coins dating back to 390 BC and graced with the head of Alexander the Great."

"I take it those are valuable? Did they arrest you?"

"To say the least." Erik frowned. "Well, no arrest per se. They made a deal with me in the end. After grilling me for a whole day — all about artifacts, the history of the area, the UNESCO convention — they actually offered me a job." He glanced at Baldwin. "Can you believe that? I was to provide intelligence on networks of antiquity thieves in Turkey, Bulgaria and northeastern Greece."

"You took the deal?"

"I had to. They would have prosecuted me if I didn't agree, hence the near miss at the border again this time. They work reasonably close with their equivalents in the Bulgarian and Greek governments, so I can work there as well."

Baldwin took all of this in and took a sip of his own water. "So all this stuff at the market … what was that? And that man at the train station was from MIT?" The questions were flying out now.

Baldwin took another sip. He was thinking, *This is so cool!* But then he remembered the concern on his father's face at the border and in the market, and that this was something that was also very serious. He had an understandable suspicion — *He hasn't told me everything yet!*

"Yes, he had to provide my clearance. I phoned him in advance but he was stuck in traffic near the old Atatürk Airport the day we arrived."

"And there's an operation going on now?"

Erik nodded. "There are Europol agents and other freelancers tied to MIT who are trying to get me to help them again. The station man, the market woman. Construction of a new light rail station near Sirkeci Station has been delayed for over a year by archaeological finds. Some artifacts have already gone missing, despite the government's best efforts. They want my help to find them."

"Will you help them?"

"Not if I can get away. They still pay me a pittance and I can make more money elsewhere. Besides, I want to accompany you to Greece. I have a treasure there that I'd like to show you."

"A treasure? What—"

"You'll just have to wait and see."

"Well, I could use a break from busy cities. Can we leave soon, maybe tomorrow?"

Erik looked pleased. "There's a bus we can take in the morning," he said with a smile.

It was just before noon the next morning when their bus pulled into the station near Kavala in Greece, just east of Thessaloniki. They disembarked, Baldwin noticing the abrupt presence of the mountains immediately to the north of the flat coastal plain where the ancient provinces of Thrace and Macedonia kiss and merge. Erik retrieved his battered old Citroën from the rear of the lot and soon had them through the streets and aboard an efficiently run ferry, heading south to a fairly large island. The warm late-summer sun brought out brilliant hues of blue sky, the lighter shades painted onto the floors of the ferries blending into the deep blues of the sea, and darker, more smoky shades marking the mountainous shorelands in the distance.

Erik pointed westward from the ferry. "That's Mount Athos over there on the eastern finger of the Halkidiki. Beautiful monasteries, quite peaceful."

"And we're going to…?"

"Thasos. It's a fair-sized island, bigger than some of the more popular Aegean Islands, but much smaller than Rhodes or Crete. It'll take us a little less than an hour to get to the southwestern coast."

Already the island coming into view looked gorgeous, with turquoise colours blending into the cliffs marking the eastern side of the island as they were pulling up to the modest-sized port town.

"And this town is called?" Baldwin had no shortage of questions. He was excited about Greece.

"Thasos as well."

"Okay, and the treasure you told me about?"

"Patience, Baldwin." Erik laughed. "Patience. You'll see."

He went to a plastic shelf near the seating area of the ferry, found a map of the island and handed it to Baldwin. "Here you go, Map Boy."

Baldwin smiled at this moniker he'd heard his Oncle Marcel use once or twice back home. He thought of home and missed his family and…

"We're going over here." His father pointed toward Limenaria on the left side of the map, the second largest town of the island.

Ten minutes later, they disembarked and Erik drove the Citroën south down the western coastal road past pleasant vistas, quaint villages and olive groves. Baldwin could feel the layers of stress disappear as he peered out the car window, kicking his sandals off and sipping on the watery remains of a café frappé he'd ordered on the ferry. As he drove, Erik explained that Thasos attracted more tourists and visitors from Eastern Europe: Bulgarians, Romanians, Croats, Poles and Serbs. The monied Western European tourists were a rare sight, sticking mainly to scenic Santorini or the party islands of Ios or Mykonos.

"That's one of the things I like most here, no Brits demanding fish and chips, very few loutish Germans, and no Americans — they don't have a McDonalds here." Erik winked as he mentioned this last point.

Baldwin laughed, and Erik shared an anecdote of how, at the height of the Gulf War in the early nineties, the refusal of the French to involve themselves in Iraq led to a US campaign to rename French fries "freedom fries."

"It was the height of idiocy and ignorance," Erik said.

And here Baldwin did his best Oncle Etienne impression. "*Frieten* were invented by the Belgians!"

This had Erik in tears laughing. "I almost miss the old goat," Erik admitted quietly after the merriment ebbed.

Rounding a hairpin bend, they came within sight of a modern hotel offering a sales showroom for gold jewellery. This was soon followed by a sign announcing a complex of stone houses. Erik signalled and turned in, following a narrow dirt lane past an abandoned Datsun pickup truck from the early 1970s, and through a wrought-iron gate to a stone-cobbled lower courtyard.

"What's this place?" Baldwin asked, all the while staring at the well-tended gardens and exotic kiwi trees bordering the parking area.

"This is part of my treasure I wanted to show you," Erik replied, pleased to see how Baldwin's face already seemed to appreciate his surroundings. "You like?"

"'t is *heel mooi*! Beautiful!" He answered without any hesitation.

Gathering his small pack, Erik led Baldwin up a steep cobbled slope along a walled walkway, all stone in a pleasing neutral grey, enhancing the fine wooden lines of walnut-brown doors, windows and shutters in the attractive buildings that formed a tree-shaded complex. Each of the houses was blessed with terraces, pergolas and orientation so as to maximize privacy and to enhance the view of the Aegean, which Baldwin noticed over his shoulder. Once he turned around and took it all in, he was delighted.

"Er ... Father, it's amazing!" Erik beamed with pleasure as it was the first time since their reunion that Baldwin had called him that. "This place is gorgeous! Why would you ever leave?"

"Yes, it's quite something, isn't it? But first, please, let me do something that I've wanted to do for a long time. I think I'm ready if you are. Come give your old boy a hug."

Baldwin didn't need any further prompting. He was over the initial shock of meeting his father after eighteen years. He'd digested most of the answers to his questions about their recent adventures. He stood receptive in the glow of the sun on the timeless stones of this magnificent place, and he felt that fate would not be so cruel as to remove what had finally been offered to him, a father. They gave each other a long, warm hug, both with tears in their eyes, released for a few moments to look each other in the face, and hugged again.

Baldwin was overcome with emotion. "Er ... Fath—"

"Shhh," said Erik, "enough with that, we're not in an old-school textbook. Please call me 'Papa.'"

"Okay ...er ... okay, Papa!" Baldwin beamed and wiped the tears out of his eyes with the back of his wrists.

"Listen," Erik said. "I still have to pay the rent and the bills too, you know. We can stay here for a couple weeks. I'll check with the owner to clear it, but that shouldn't be an issue, they live here in the first building with the gardens."

Over the next few days, father and son explored some of the most beautifully set beaches on the island. During the evenings, they feasted on delicious meals of fresh fish and olives, Greek salads and, one night, a more traditional meal of moussaka, all splashed down with the delightful anise-flavoured Greek ouzo.

On their first visit to their local beach near Limenaria, Erik smiled and said, "This is the second part of my treasure!"

Deeply appreciative of the full beach view, Baldwin loved the migration of colours from white sand to turquoise to aquamarine to a navy-blue Mount Athos on the steely grey-blue horizon. A white triangle of a sailboat moved slowly in the distance. It was so very peaceful! He couldn't wait to wade in and enjoy the coolness of the Aegean, washing away all the worries in the world.

One evening, they decided to stay in, having had a substantial lunch earlier in the day. Instead, they were content to peck away at kalamata olives, feta cheese and a fresh loaf of olive bread, the owner being very generous to their guests. They sat on an elevated balcony and, soon after dark, the splendour of the Milky Way opened up before their eyes, brilliant in the wide sky, far away from the distraction of city lights and noise.

Erik went into the house briefly and returned with a Schweppes pop bottle filled with a golden-brown liquid. With a twinkle in his eye, Erik poured them each a small glass and raised his own up for a toast.

"Baldwin, I can't describe the joy you have brought me in even these few short weeks!"

"Me too — I mean, this has been great." He watched in curiosity as Erik twisted the cap off and set it on the table. Vapours of a strong spirit wafted toward Baldwin. "What's in the bottle? Smells a bit like something a lady had me taste on the train."

"It's Bulgarian rakia. Carefully made by a kind man I know. You may remember him. He was sitting in the café in Veliko Tarnovo with a newspaper, drinking a beer. Do you recall?"

"I think … oh, he was joined by the woman with the kids, one with a yo-yo. I swear I saw them everywhere."

"That man is my eyes and ears at the airport in Sofia where he works as an aircraft mechanic, as good as gold he is. I once helped him repair the latch on the trunk of his car; he repaid me with this bottle. It's great stuff, very powerful though. Let's toast!"

And they did. To each other. To Oncle Marcel and Tante Viv. To the Flemish. To Bulgaria where they met. Even to the olives and feta, as good an excuse as any. They toasted in a half a dozen languages that they knew at least the word for *Cheers!*: *Yamas! Santé! Saludo! Prost!* And, in honour of the rakia, *Nazdrave!* — "To your health!" in Bulgarian.

They watched the stars in silence for a few minutes, Erik finally filling in the pensive gap. "So, in Damme, is there someone waiting for you? Did you break anyone's heart by leaving on your adventure?"

Baldwin looked up slowly, then looked up higher, at Orion's Belt, and blew a short whoosh of air out of his mouth, turning to Erik and looking him in the eye.

"Yes — er, no … it's a bit complicated," he opened tentatively.

"Try me. I have lots of time for you. Eighteen years to catch up," Erik countered and smiled as he teasingly threw his son's words back at him.

Baldwin began again, slowly and softly. "About eighteen months ago, I ended a relationship with my first girlfriend. We were schoolmates but … I guess we just outgrew each other."

"That doesn't sound so complicated."

"Well, that's not the full story."

Erik said nothing, his turn to use silence to draw out his son.

"Okay, do you recall I mentioned Remi is together with someone?" he started.

"Yes."

"Well, just as you did, he fell for a Walloon, a girl named Yvonne from Liège whose parents moved to Brugge — 'Bruges' as she insists on calling it — a transfer from the post office."

Place names in Belgium, a country that was devised in the opinion of some as a post-Napoleanic buffer state between the European great powers, ran symbolic in the daily lives of Flemish and Walloon Belgian citizens. Both jockeyed for their own idea of language fairness. Baldwin's revelation, that he was aware of his mother's origins, was not lost on Erik. Baldwin pronounced *Brugge* in the throaty Flemish dialect, "Bruh-ha."

"You knew your mother was also from a Walloon family, from Namur?" Erik said, surprised.

"Tante Vivienne filled me in on the whole family tree. She used to speak to me in French — a good reason I think why I can manage French and Flemish without problems..." Here Baldwin looked away to the stars for a short while before he continued. "She's very special Yvonne. We have recently ... well, at least I have recently realized how special."

Erik was silent for a few moments, but finally spoke up. "And have you shared this with her? Or is it just you?"

"Sort of — I mean we've talked of course, but she's careful and I can't blame her." He reached out with his glass as Erik offered a top-up from the bottle of rakia. "She doesn't want to hurt Remi. And I don't either," he said while stifling a mild belch that watered his eyes. *Mô, this stuff is strong*, he thought. "But in those last few weeks before I left, even when she didn't say anything, it felt like we were talking. Someone would crack a joke and we'd look at each other ... and her eyes, they're so beautiful! It's almost as if — well I'm not sure what she's feeling, but once she said, '*Tu as de beaux yeux.*'"

Erik smiled. "That definitely sounds like she's flirting. Most people save those kinds of compliments for their sweethearts."

Baldwin felt a little warm. It was strange to talk to someone about this, but it was also something he realized he'd been missing in his life, a father to turn to when he had something on his mind. "I can only believe what her eyes are telling me. I know she wouldn't lead me on, she's not like that. She's actually a very honest, matter-of-fact person, more reasons I like her so much." He looked up at the sky again. "I'm one of the most impatient people in the world, but it's not easy to see her with him when I get these signs that she wants to be with me."

Erik was proud that his son had fully opened up to him. He felt a slight twinge of guilt that he still had a chance to become so close to a son he never knew until recently due to choices he had made when not too much older than Baldwin. Not wanting to leave the opportunity hanging, he added, "You're sure this isn't just infatuation? I mean, you're not just being a guy with a beautiful girl who told him he has nice eyes?"

Baldwin looked down from the stars, wondering if he'd left his common sense up there among the heavens, turned and looked his father in the eyes.

"She's beautiful, yes, very athletic. But, no. This is beyond infatuation, for me at least. For her, I don't know — she may decide I'm not for her and move on to someone else if it doesn't work out with Remi. But I don't see them together much longer anyway. He does too many stupid things. He doesn't respect her like I would. And he's been hanging around with dockyard crews in Zeebrugge and with Oncle Etienne, moonlighting on the side from his railway job. The thing is, they're together, and for me, life is too short to pine away forever…"

"So you'll try to get together when you go home?"

"I don't know. It's not easy with Remi around. If they're still together, well then, she'll have to make a decision. Or Remi's going to get suspicious. I wonder sometimes if he's already." Baldwin leaned forward and adjusted the small pillow he had in the small of his back. He felt like he was on the edge of sharing perhaps a little too much.

Erik recognized his level of unease and his movements to buy a little time to contemplate. He switched topics slightly to coping and well-being. "You must be tied in knots sometimes. How do you handle it?"

"I run. I keep busy." Baldwin shrugged slightly, staring at his glass and looking as though he had the weight of the world on his mind, his heart his own personal Atlas.

Out of empathy, Erik left a few moments before adding, "And in the end?"

"I'm not ready to give up on her, but — well, time will tell."

Erik nodded. "The world's most impatient man feels he must be patient because it's worth having what he has and not hurting those close to him. He survives in the meantime by communicating with his eyes." He smiled at his son.

They raised a glass of rakia to a future unknown.

By now Baldwin was feeling the effects of the rakia, but in a pleasant way. Initially he was feeling quite vulnerable but now more comfortable after spilling his inner thoughts. He opened up further with something that had been on his mind since first seeing his father, exploring another belief he held strongly.

"Papa, you know that beyond maybe a month or so, I'll have to return home."

"*Ja* … I'd assumed that the funds were not limitless."

Baldwin looked away, as if another glimpse at Orion's Belt would give him the courage to ask his next question. "Why don't you come home with me?"

Erik held his glass midway to his lips and his breath inside his chest. He slowly expelled it and took a sip of rakia.

"I … I have my business here … that issue with your Oncle Etienne … what would I do? This is something I'd really have to think about as … I don't believe—"

Baldwin set his glass down with a clank that interrupted this response. He took a breath, his face earnest and serious and blurted out clearly, not wanting any excuse to separate him from his father again. "Well, I believe!"

PART 3

THE GREAT COIN CAPER

It was late summer in the covered market in the old quarter of Istanbul. A blond-haired boy and his brother had just picked up a postcard showing a lovely white panoramic landscape. Their mother had bought it for them along with a stamp so that they could send it to their great-uncle in the UK, and in part as a reward for their patience while she picked out souvenirs, an eclectic mix of Turkish delight, small embroidered purses and a jar of ground spicy red pepper.

Sadie D'Arnaud was middle-class English and had married well. She'd put off this trip with her boys for many years, waiting until Romy and Guy were old enough to remember the experience. It had originally been planned for the whole family based on a Christmastime promise, but a faulty gas valve in a restaurant kitchen took the life of her French husband, Gustave. And that changed everything.

Sadie and the boys were left with a generous insurance settlement. This compensation, together with an annuity from Gustave's family estate in Burgundy, left them comfortably well off and allowed Sadie to "push the boat out," to take the eager boys out of their school for two terms to fulfill the promised family voyage.

She was a slender woman with auburn hair worn in a neck-length bob. She had an impressive sense of style, wearing dresses and skirts despite the challenges this sometimes presented while travelling. The boys were both as blond as their father had been. She saw his features in their faces every day, which gave her some comfort that, in a way, he was still along for the journey.

"Is this snow, Mom?" Guy, her youngest, ten years old aspiring to teenhood, posed the question.

"No, it's a white rock formation, Pamukkale. We'll be going there in a couple days."

"Sweet! Can you skate on it?"

"I don't think so."

"Why? Why are we going there then?" asked Romy. He was slightly taller than Guy and had just turned twelve.

"It's not flat ... Are you hungry? Look, a doner kebab stand."

They ordered and moaned out load at the delectable treat. Guy sat on a small stool and licked his fingers after devouring his, famished after eating only melon for breakfast and picking at his dinner of fish the night before. Finished before the others in his family, and setting his stuffed monkey aside, he began to play with his new top. As happened on occasion, the top spun at a strange angle, rolling behind a small pavement bollard. As he went to pick it up, he sidestepped two men ordering a drink and noticed a skinny young woman running with her dreadlocked male partner. When she was close to him, she threw a small sack near his feet, beside the top, and said in a low voice, "Little darling, please hide these. I'll see you soon." Charmed by the attention and without thinking, Guy quickly hid the bag behind the monkey. Noticing his response, she then threw back her head to Dreadlocks and spouted, "Remember the monkey, kid!" They both then dashed three stalls away, hiding behind a thick collection of hanging carpets with a narrow vantage point to watch the boy.

Guy took the small sack, undid the drawstring and peered inside at two gold coins, one with the head of a rather handsome man with a crown of laurel leaves. Knowing he had something extraordinary, but not knowing what to do with it, he was of two minds. Tell his mother or hold back his sneaky conversation with the strange skinny woman. An innocent free spirit enjoying his adventure with little understanding of the consequences, he slipped the whole sack into an open seam that had worked its way loose in his stuffed monkey, his own little bit of intrigue from a trip to this very odd place where his mother had brought him. Dreadlocks and Skinny Woman watched closely through a gap in the hanging carpets, then bolted in the other direction at the approaching sound of a police siren.

Olof Vinter didn't look Swedish, nor did he particularly enjoy the name he was given at birth by his father. Born in Baku to an Azerbaijani mother, he was moved from the Swedish Embassy and official residence at ten years old to Stockholm, where he soon learned that he was different — and had numerous bloody noses in the schoolyard to prove it. Immersing himself in books on Asian history in fidelity to his land of birth, he soon grew tired of the ignorance of his classmates in high school over matters of geopolitics in southern Asia, the arts, culture and language differences. A loner, he focused on his studies and martial arts, which he learned from a half-Armenian sensei in the spartan basement of a battered building in Kungsholmen. Unlike the bulk of his senior class, he had the light-olive skin and jet-black hair of his homeland, caterpillar eyebrows nearly knit together over the bridge of his nose. He was lean and muscular like his father, but had the hands and facial features of his mother. By the time he graduated, his disruptive behaviour at home led his father to pack him off to Heidelberg, Germany, to complete his education. Fed up with the conservative views in the German south, he quit and moved to Berlin, joining the underworld, and within three weeks, he walked out of a bank with a stolen handgun and a knapsack full of euros.

On a rooftop terrace overlooking Istiklal, the busy shopping street in the Beyoglu quarter of Istanbul, the boys were taking turns alternately hugging and trying to tear the stuffed monkey out of each other's hands. Neither noticed a skinny woman wearing sunglasses, seated at the far end of the elevated patio nursing a Turkish coffee and feigning to speak on her mobile, covertly watching their antics. Soon the game became out of hand, and an errant throw sent the monkey sliding over the guard railing down into the street below. With a wail, the boys dashed to see what had become of him, all the while blaming each other for the mishap.

"Now look! He's gone! I can't believe this! It's your fault!"

"No, it's yours!"

Sadie took their hands and stood between them looking over the rail. "Never mind blaming, boys. Where did he land?"

"He fell in a truck going by! We gotta get him back!"

"Oh no! What rotten luck. I'm so sorry, honey."

"It was a red truck, with carpets in the back, like we saw in the market when that guy kept trying to give us apple tea," Romy said as he looked at the road below once more, hoping to catch a glimpse.

A kind man sitting nearby had seen the act play out and offered some help. "The truck had writing on it, *Ozil* ... like the German football player, that's why I remember it. *Ozil Kilim Nevşeh* ... or something like that."

Sadie thought for a moment as one of the words sounded somewhat familiar. "*Kilim* is a type of carpet."

The man, suddenly inspired, was even more helpful. "*Nevşeh* is probably Nevşehir, in Cappadocia, you think so?"

She thanked the man and hugged her sons, excitedly. "I bet that truck is going to a carpet shop in the town where we were planning to go anyway! Ha! We now have a mission! You boys kept moaning and asking why we were going to the middle of Turkey for carpets and now we have another reason! We're going to find Maimuna!"

Somewhat mollified, young Guy was not yet fully convinced of ever seeing the monkey again, or the coins he'd stashed inside.

Skinny Woman observed the whole exchange and quietly spoke on her mobile before heading to the toilets. The Turkish coffee didn't agree with her constitution. She ran the last bit and cursed the lack of availability of her favourite *café con leche*, and cursed even more the reasons that she'd chosen to leave her native Spain.

Erik and Baldwin had only just packed their rucksacks for the morning ferry to the Greek mainland when Erik's mobile rang. While he was occupied, Baldwin went out on the terrace for a last look at one of the most peaceful scenes he'd experienced in his whole life, the Aegean looking west from the island of Thasos. It was late September, and only the night before, his father had agreed to return with him to Belgium. His thoughts were far away, on someone he missed at home, a riff and lyrics from a Snow Patrol track playing in his head — something about lying down together and forgetting about everything else. He heard a noise and turned around.

Erik stood in the doorway, looking pale and concerned. "We have a problem," he said, a grim look on his weathered face.

"What's the matter?"

"The police are on their way. We must wait here until they arrive."

"But—"

"Yes, we'll have to miss the first ferry. They said they'd be here in fifteen minutes."

"Did they say what they want? Are we in trouble?"

"They didn't tell me anything, just for us to stay put."

"Us? They know I'm with you?" Baldwin was nonplussed, somewhere between puzzled and annoyed that his father may not have shared everything during their moonlight chat.

"Evidently," Erik muttered, in resignation.

Olof took a cheap bucket flight to Belgrade, the first flight available from Tegel Airport following his Berlin bank heist. In Belgrade, he boarded a train to Sofia, and that very evening jimmied the door of an antique shop, making off with a chalice, an icon and a golden, gem-encrusted crucifix. His intent was to pawn them in Istanbul, his next destination, and to get to know the antiquity scene in the city's old quarter.

The boys and their mother boarded an overnight bus from the Gülhane Park Hotel, bound for Kuşadasi on the Aegean coast. They wanted to explore the ancient Roman city of Ephesus on their way to Cappadocia. They didn't notice the swarthy man with the deep-set eyes and bushy moustache wearing a red vest and fez, serving ice cream as bait for tourists. He watched them board the bus and, using his mobile, made a discreet call.

Baldwin's mind raced. What could lead to a police visit? Did his father tell him everything about his clandestine work? Was there a problem with the Turkish police again?

He watched his father text messaging from another mobile he'd withdrawn from above a beam that spanned the ceiling of the stone house. Once completed, Erik took out the SIM card and flushed it down the toilet, then threw the phone into a thorn bush among a copse of ageless olive trees on a steep slope behind the house. Baldwin's silent inquiry was met with a response he was starting to recognize too well — the "not now, I'll explain later" stone-faced look of his father.

A dark sedan pulled into the courtyard five minutes later. Erik went to greet them, waved away the curious landlord and walked into the house with two officers in dark jackets and slacks.

Motioning for Erik and Baldwin to sit down at the dining table, the first agent, a heavy-set middle-aged man with a rather fleshy face and large nose, introduced himself as Agent Costos and pointed at his partner, a slim man in his thirties, indicating him to be Agent Petras. With no hint of request or apology, Petras started to search around the house, opening drawers, lifting sofa cushions, inspecting around light fixtures and behind artwork.

Erik spoke up in annoyance. "What's all this? Why have you come?"

Agent Costos leaned his substantial frame on the edge of the kitchen counter, not taking his eyes off the man and his son, while Petras continued, unfazed.

"We have a complex situation that poses more questions than answers at this point, a couple matters requiring us to investigate. To start, do you recall your little caper of some five and a half years ago, a trip from Varna to Istanbul?" Costos asked.

"How can I forget? Your counterparts in MIT remind me constantly," Erik replied, irked.

"Then you'll remember the nature of your precious cargo during that incident?"

"Yes ... coins ... Thracian, from the third century BC, if my memory serves me well."

"Exactly. Well, both of these coins have somehow eluded the MIT once more," Costos continued, without a hint of contrition.

"And how is that my issue? I don't have them."

"You claim not to have them. Okay for now."

Costos got up and checked to see if there was any coffee in the carafe on the counter. Disappointment registered on his face as it was empty, so he returned to face the table, removing an envelope from the inside breast pocket of his jacket. From the envelope, he pulled out a series of photos, and with his pudgy fingers, he spread them out on the dining table, photo side down.

"The second matter is more time critical. Can you assure me that you were travelling alone in Istanbul?"

"We were. I was showing Baldwin … my son, Baldwin, around the city … and then we came here to Greece."

"There were no diversions? Others met? Perhaps over on the Asian side?"

"No. Just the two of us."

"And you were with your … son … the whole time?"

"Yes," he replied tersely.

"Perhaps your young companion, er, son, may have further information, hmm?"

This question left both Erik and Baldwin puzzled, not knowing where it was headed and for what reason.

"My son knows nothing of this whole situation with the coins," Erik insisted.

"Well, why don't we have a little discussion and see, hmm?" Costos pressed.

Intently staring at Baldwin, Costos took an accusatory tone. "You said you were travelling alone, but I've come to learn of other companions. A women and two boys who you appear to have spent some time with here and there." Costos was stone-faced in providing this information, hoping to elicit a response from Baldwin.

For dramatic effect, he slowly turned over passport-sized photos of them all, each looking straight-faced and uncomfortable in their effort to obey the arcane rules of passport-photo imaging. Baldwin couldn't place the photos until he saw one of the boy who had the yo-yo, but he said nothing and shook his head, still uncertain where the questions were going.

"You claim not to know them?" Costos restarted the interrogation.

"Correct. I don't know them." Baldwin held firm.

"How do you explain this then?" Costos turned over what he thought would be his trump card, another larger photo he extracted from his breast pocket. It showed a surveillance camera image of Erik and Baldwin standing at a kebab vendor near the market in Istanbul. Seated in front was the slender woman with the auburn hair in a print dress and the two blond-haired boys that Baldwin had seen a few different times during his travels. The younger boy was clutching a doner in one hand and a stuffed red-and-gold monkey in the other. The second boy had a yo-yo. Baldwin, now rattled that he found himself under such close surveillance, spoke up in protest.

"This photo doesn't show that we know them, which we don't. It shows only that we were ordering a drink near the covered market! What's all this about anyway?"

At this point, Agent Petras opened the door, revealing Baldwin's disassembled backpack on the front walk behind him. He entered the room holding Baldwin's camera and beckoned his partner away so he could speak quietly in the man's ear — a bushy one with sprouts of hair protruding out of it, keeping the younger partner at a measured distance.

With new information, Costos returned to them. "Your protests are becoming quite interesting, my young man. Perhaps you care to explain this photo" — here he held up Baldwin's digital camera — "from what appears to be the Nevski Cathedral in Sofia, if I'm not mistaken?"

Baldwin looked at his camera, evidently searched from beginning to end by the persistent Petras. On the display screen was the self-portrait he'd taken where the mother and boys were crossing in front of the cathedral in the backdrop of his photo.

"Another coincidence then? You must take us for fools, young Dutchman, always so clever," Costos said in scorn.

"Flemish ... it doesn't matter. I'm telling you, I don't know them, okay? They must have been travelling the same route. It's a coincidence," replied Baldwin.

"No, not okay!" Costos's voice became more heated. "The woman and her boys are now travelling into the interior of Turkey, we believe! And the coins have gone missing, and I want to know what you know so that we can find them all!"

"But we've told you all we know!"

The younger agent, Petras, now spoke up. It soon became evident from his manner and tone that he was actually the senior officer of the two. He spoke directly to Erik in a grave voice. "You're evidently very resourceful, and based on discussions with our Turkish counterparts at MIT, I'm authorized to make one concession … to give you a chance. Here's the deal: You have two weeks to find this family and those coins and provide us full information daily. If you fail in either, you'll be sitting in a Turkish jail awaiting trial for your little mishap of five years ago. And as for your young Dutch son here, he'll be held for further questioning in the disappearance of these others … and charges may be pending."

"Flemish," Baldwin blurted. "But what—"

"My son and I will take the deal," Erik said over him.

Agents Petras and Costos gave them a mobile number to call for their daily report and drove off in search of a coffee.

The waif of a woman had been no help. She fainted almost immediately, but Funar Grigorescu had just finished extracting the information he needed from the frightened young man with dreadlocks — "We gave it to a blond boy with a toy stuffed monkey!" — when he heard the tinkle of the bell announcing entry into his pawn shop in the Aksaray quarter. With a quick chop to the neck, the aging street fighter knocked Dreadlocks unconscious. Then he wiped his hands on a towel and came into the shop from the back room, firmly closing the door behind him. In the front, near a display case of coins, he saw the silhouette of someone against the shop window, filthy as it was and covered with posters.

Olof, dressed in a dark-green crew neck shirt and black blazer, would have looked rather business-like if it weren't for the heavy Doc Martens boots he chose to wear despite the heat of Istanbul.

Funar approached the young man. "*Yardımcı olabilir miyim?* Can I help you?" He said both in Turkish and English with a heavy Romanian accent, not knowing the origin of the new punter, and as if the last thing in the world he was providing was an earnest offer of help.

Olof was not put off. "I search for coins, coins of high value," he said in clipped English.

"This is pawn shop, not antique shop or museum. These over here come from Ottoman Empire. These others are lira from 1950s and these back to when Atatürk in power," Funar offered.

The coins were under a glass countertop in open ceramic bowls, jumbled together, many with their elaborate calligraphy discoloured from exposure. A numismatic failure of proper storage.

"No, I'm looking for old examples. My contact in Germany told me to search for Funar. You're Funar, aren't you?"

The Romanian, who had gone by this one name over the years out of simplicity, immediately backed up, grabbed a heavy brass statue of a rearing horse and stared at Olof menacingly. "Who sent you? Who are you?"

"Well, I'm no relation to that poor kid in the back I can tell you. I'm Olof. Augustus in Leipzig gave me your name."

"How do you know about shaggy boy in back?" Funar shouted, feeling a mix of puzzlement and frustration. He did not like to be caught with less information on his actions than anyone he encountered in life.

"I saw you following him and his tidy little piece near the Egyptian column yesterday, after the police released them. And fifteen minutes ago I could hear his screams from the miserable room I rented next door above the café. Rather than wait any longer, I thought I'd approach you. Augustus said you were looking for help," replied Olof in a manner that said he couldn't care less about Funar's bluster.

"Augustus. How do I know we speak of same man? What is code line? You are supposed to know it."

"The line is, 'I really like pork sausages.' Why he picked that I don't know. The man looks like a shrivelled sausage in that old suit of his. Probably hates Muslims."

Funar put the statue down, lit a Maltepe cigarette and looked at Olof appraisingly. Old thug sizing up new thug.

"You should learn some respect, young man. The Nazis took his whole family when he was younger, his farm, his home, everything! What the Nazis didn't take, the Stasi squeezed him for their own purposes."

"I see," said Olof with a degree of remorse. "I meant no disrespect."

"Well then, so now you know. And the coin story?" Funar was eager to move on to business.

"If we're talking about the same coins, yes, Thracian, third century BC. Augustus told me that a drop-off in Taksim Square some five years ago went sideways, MIT was tipped off, some Belgian guy got strung up, and MIT subsequently lost the package almost as soon as they brought it back to their station as evidence."

"Was not lost. I have a man in evidence holding area. He brought to me for handsome price."

"So you had them? And?"

Funar motioned to the room in the back. "Shaggy *kanal scheisser* stole from my storage locker. I tell woman I know who does things for MIT, she tells Belgian guy she work with, same one as five years ago, but he does not help, instead sends for police. They give coins in pouch to small tourist boy with toy monkey. Police in sweep of market pick up Dreadlocks and Skinny Woman. They say nothing and are released — no evidence. I find them in Taksim Square and bring them here."

"This is what you got out of the kid in back?" Olof asked.

"Yes."

"So we need to find the monkey kid."

"Yes, need monkey kid, but I cannot leave here, contracts, business, Istanbul. This why I ask Augustus for help. He sends me you, who probably know no Turkish. Big help!" he threw in sarcastically.

Olof looked up at Funar and stared him directly in his tired eyes. One was just recovering from bloodshot. He'd had enough of this treatment. "Listen, old man. I can speak Turkish, as well as German, Swedish, Greek, English and Azerbaijani. Good enough for you?"

"What is good for Azerbaijani?"

"And you ask me to show some respect! How much will you pay me?" Olof demanded.

"You recover, you get twenty percent of value."

"Seriously? Twenty percent? That's a relationship starting out well, isn't it? You'll never find them if this monkey kid and family move on. I want fifty percent." Olof continued to stare at Funar.

Funar looked his fifty-eight years. While still tough as nails, he no longer had the energy for pursuit in the field.

"Okay, okay, but you must get rid of Shaggy Boy and the skinny woman for me. Drop in Bosphorus. I don't care." Funar, always the negotiator.

"Consider it done. I'll take care of it and then search the hotels for descriptions of the monkey kid."

"Fine. You cover your own travel costs," Funar threw out.

"As I suspected. Take me to them," Olof said.

Olof had selective scruples. He wasn't a murderer, at least not yet, and he wasn't about to do the old man's dirty work for him. He quickly found Dreadlocks, who looked alarmed, and gave him a stiff punch in the head to preclude any notion of escape. He then had the young couple, evidently Spanish from the numbers called on her mobile, drugged and docile, put in the back of a Volkswagen estate car he'd hotwired from a long-term parking lot near the airport. He lost no time and drove that morning over to Üsküdar, on the the Asian side of Istanbul, and propped them on a park bench behind a small mosque. He left a menacing note in Spanish in Dreadlock's front pocket:

Leave Turkey or next time you will not wake up!!

Just as he returned to the driver's seat, his mobile vibrated and, picking up the call, he heard the guttural voice of his ice cream man with a fez.

Using his network of contacts, it didn't take Erik long to learn that the boys and their mother were last seen boarding a package bus to Anatolia, the Asian mainland of Turkey. Erik cleared the Turkish border without incident, waved through by an impatient inspector. A car in the next lane had blown a radiator hose and was sending clouds of steam over the neighbouring platform. Erik thought ahead as he drove past Edirne toward Istanbul, Baldwin dozing in the passenger seat until his mobile buzzed. He blinked a few times, holding up his phone in a bit of a daze as he read the message — then deleted it almost immediately — and said more to himself than anyone in particular, "How is anyone expected to communicate anything delicate through a text?"

Erik, bored with the slow movement of a truck in front of him, picked up the thought. "All good at home? You must be missing your family and friends."

"Not really. I could sit beside most of them again tomorrow and they'd ask one question about my trip and then start talking about the World Cup without missing a beat."

Erik nodded at the mobile, prying some more. "Any changes? Your thoughts." Erik was Flemish in his directness without knowing where he should probably stop pressing.

"No, just 'hey this' and 'hey that.'" Baldwin shifted in his seat. "I feel the same way about things as the day I left. Just wish someone would invent an emoji that said, 'Wish I could spend even ten minutes with you.'"

"Maybe you should invent one."

Baldwin laughed. "Maybe I will. A colon for eyes and a sideways number ten below."

"It would look like someone with a pointy nose."

"Ha! Perfect for me!"

They both laughed at this, and then spent a long ten minutes staring at a truck that finally changed over to the slow lane ahead, leaving them to advance to the next truck in front.

The mother and boys got a giggle over posing for silly photos in the preserved Roman latrine at Ephesus and were walking to explore the Library of Celsus. A man in a green shirt, black blazer and Doc Martens watched them, his eyes hard-wired for signs of a stuffed monkey.

They will have to be questioned, he thought.

Erik and Baldwin passed a signpost with distances for İznik, Bursa, İzmir and Kuşadasi.

"I'm afraid we have a lot of ground yet to cover, son, and they have almost two days on us."

"It's all right. Let me know if you want me to help with the drive."

"I may take you up on that, maybe near İzmir."

"Strange-sounding names. I was so fixed on Istanbul growing up, I never noticed the names of other places, except maybe Ankara, the capital."

"Well, depending what period you were reading about, they may have had other names. Some were Greek cities, at least Greek in population."

"Greek?"

"Yes, in the period after the First World War, the Greeks and Turks were at each other's throats. There was a large Greek minority in Turkey and a large Turkish minority in Greece, former Hellenic period settlements in the case of the former, the legacy of the Ottoman Empire for the latter," Erik spelled out.

"So they kicked each other out?"

"More or less. The Turks cleared out Cappadocia and all former Orthodox churches became museums, pensions, houses. Even some hermit's caves became stables."

"And these other places?"

"Smyrna, famous for its ceramic tiles, became İzmir. Adrianople, the city named after the Roman Emperor Hadrian, became Edirne. İznik, which we just passed near, was Nicaea, which you may recognize as the name of the famous Nicene Creed proclaiming the beliefs of the Catholic Church. Thereafter, naming Jesus as mortal or anything but part of the Divine Trilogy became heresy. Other cities like Antioch became Antakya. The list goes on."

"And the Greeks expelled Turks?"

"Oh, yes. Thousands of them. The whole thing was a bitter, bloody affair. Many were killed in spite and revenge on both sides.

Atatürk sealed the deal to instill a new Turkish nationhood by renaming Constantinople 'Istanbul' and moving the capital to Ankara, a backwater of punishment on the international diplomatic circuit. Imagine being posted there after the energy of Istanbul?"

"I guess it would suck," Baldwin mused. He had minimal understanding of what life would be like in the diplomatic world.

Baldwin texted his Oncle Marcel in Damme on his change in itinerary and settled in for another long car ride.

A man in a black blazer and green shirt approached Sadie and her boys as they exited their bus in Denizli.

"You need hostel? Come with me."

"We haven't decided yet where we're staying," said Sadie.

"It's okay, you come with me. Manny's Hostel. In your *Happy Planet* guide," he persisted.

"Oh, yes, I saw that one in there. You work there? Is it clean?"

"Yes, yes, yes, no problem. You come with me." Tired from the overnight bus and eager to find lodging and stow their baggage before exploring the nearby cliffs of Pamukkale on their postcard, she acquiesced to this persistent, annoying man and they loaded their packs into the back of his Volkswagen. As always, she kept her small purse, meaning to write the postcard with the boys.

Olof quietly drove to an older building on the edge of town. Once they arrived, he told them to leave their packs in the car. "You can retrieve them, or I can have a local boy retrieve them for you once we get you settled," he offered. A true scam artist preying on their uncertainty. Sadie glanced at the front of the building. It looked clean enough with a sign that said Manny's. A modest entrance door was framed with a flower box on one side and a yellow Turkish post box on the other.

Olof led them through the lobby, where a deserted front desk was littered with travel pamphlets and an open calendar, presumably the reservation book for the hostel.

"You can rest in here while I get you booked in." He pointed to a large back room with a bench and a few chairs and a small TV set in the corner playing music videos at a low volume. They followed the man gratefully, eager to get sorted. The boys sat on the bench, but Sadie remained standing, ready to register.

The man turned and shut the door behind him. "All right, this doesn't have to be difficult. Just do as I say and no one gets hurt Which of these two boys has the monkey!"

Sadie stared in disbelief. "What? You don't work here? Who the hell are you and what do you want?" Her accent grew more posh with each word.

"You are correct. Manny's ... unfortunately ... closed yesterday. An accident in the family I'm told."

Sadie took a shaky breath. "What do you want? You're frightening the children." She instinctively stood in front of the boys to shield them, looking around the room for something, anything, she might use in the event they needed to against the man.

"As I said, just do as I say and no one gets hurt. Who has the monkey?" he pressed.

Unable to contain himself, and not wanting anything bad to happen to his family, Guy blurted out, in tears, "We don't have the monkey. The coins inside neither. It fell in a truck in Istanbul and we're hoping to get it back."

This outburst both shocked and puzzled his mother and brother.

"Guy? What coins inside?" Sadie asked, fully confused.

He was about to answer, but the man beat him to it.

"These would be the coins given to you by a skinny woman near the covered market in Istanbul, am I correct, young man?"

"Yeah," he sobbed.

"And where do you hope to get it back?"

"In Nevsha, or something like that ... some place with carpets."

At this admission, the man's eyebrows shot up. "Ah! in ... Nevşehir ... very good."

Feeling frustrated at the games this awful man was playing with her son's head, Sadie bravely stepped forward.

"Look, we're going now. And if you don't let us go immediately, I'll have the law on you. You have no right to hold us here. I suspect the Turkish police have a special way to treat those who interfere with tourists. And we know nothing of these coins."

Olof was not fazed. He reached to his right and opened a closet and onto the floor fell a man who appeared to be the hostel manager, gagged with duct tape, eyes bulging with fear, ankles and wrists bound.

Sadie jumped backward with a gasp, her arms coming protectively around her boys on either side of her.

"As I said, and I will make it plain to you one last time. Just do as I say and no one gets hurt," Olof said darkly.

While the boys and their mother recoiled and clung together in fear at the sight of this poor man, Olof dragged the manager out and shut the door, locking them in behind him.

"Mommy, I'm sorry I didn't say anything about the coins." Guy was shattered.

"Don't worry, sweetie. It's not your fault." His mother held his face in both hands and looked him in the eyes. "We'll get us out of this mess. We just need a plan." Romy gave him a supportive hug and felt bad for throwing around Maimuna on the Istanbul terrace. And with that, they pooled their thoughts before the door was again unlocked.

They were now just west of Denizli, splitting a loaf of bread and some olives they'd purchased roadside in the car. Erik hung up his mobile, exhausted from having driven through the night, and looked at Baldwin.

"My contacts tell me that a man named Olof Vinter was dispatched by an underground old timer named Funar to go after the boy. Apparently the coins were somehow stuffed inside the kid's toy monkey. I assume that's why they've fallen off the grid."

"Poor kid. He must be really scared," Baldwin muttered.

"Well, let's find them. They were headed to Nevşehir according to their bus itinerary." Erik took it in and saw that their path ahead was getting more serious than he previously anticipated. They pulled away, heading eastward for Cappadocia.

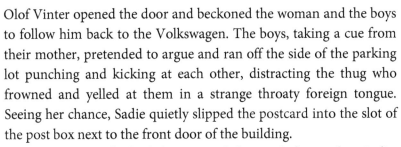

Olof Vinter opened the door and beckoned the woman and the boys to follow him back to the Volkswagen. The boys, taking a cue from their mother, pretended to argue and ran off the side of the parking lot punching and kicking at each other, distracting the thug who frowned and yelled at them in a strange throaty foreign tongue. Seeing her chance, Sadie quietly slipped the postcard into the slot of the post box next to the front door of the building.

When he finally had them rounded up, Olof turned to Sadie. "Right," he said. "You'll drive us to Nevşehir to retrieve the monkey."

"Oh, I'm from the UK," she said. "I can't drive on the right. You'll have to drive. And besides, someone has to watch and referee these two."

"Okay, fine," he said. "I will drive, but no funny business!"

The boys climbed in the backseat with their mother. Olof drove off. He didn't buckle and turned sideways occasionally and repeatedly glanced in the rearview mirror to monitor the group in the back. After two hours, they left the main motorway and entered a two-lane secondary highway, and traffic was slower and thicker as a consequence. Near Konya, Olof glanced in the rearview mirror and then stomped on the accelerator to pass a line of six cars that had held them up for forty minutes, racing for a gap that was created by a slow truck in front of the line, with an oncoming car just breaching a small hill in the distance.

Sadie sat up in alarm. "What are you doing? Are you crazy? You're going to kill us all! Where did you learn to drive?" she ripped into him, annoyed and a bit frantic.

His left hand white-knuckled the wheel, his right was ready to reach inside his jacket. He swerved into the right lane in front of the truck, just missing the oncoming car, which whizzed past blaring the horn. "In Germany," Olof muttered, "where they know how to drive!"

As he looked at her menacingly, Romy suddenly yelled "Monkey!" from behind him and rammed the back of his fist into Olof's right ear. Olof turned his head from the blow and opened his mouth wide to bark an order, but Sadie rammed two pieces of Turkish delight smothered in red-hot ground pepper into his mouth with her right hand, her left hand whacking him on the upper back over the seat, making him gulp for air.

It didn't take long for the warm, gooey candy to lodge near the back of his mouth; his eyes bulged as he clutched at his throat. With tears in his eyes clouding his vision, he quickly pulled the car over at a petrol station just inside the city limits of Konya and came to a roaring stop. Sadie hopped out, opened the driver's door and began pulling at Olof. Since he hadn't strapped in, she hauled him with a grunt, and he fell out, his face red, one hand clutching at his throat, the other sticking a finger in his mouth trying to dislodge the obstruction. The boys took turns punching him in the face, Romy bashing him repeatedly with his yo-yo in hand. As Olof fell forward, Sadie, still livid at this man who put her boys in danger, kicked him square in the groin from behind. He doubled over. They left him there gasping, climbed back in the car and drove off in search of a police station.

Anyone can learn to drive on the other side of the road given the right circumstances, Sadie thought, still shaking.

A young woman and an older man sat at the corner table in the front room of The Hare and Hounds, each immersed in their own thoughts after the briefest exchange of conversation during a mid-September squall.

This was the man's weekly night out in the English village of Chorlton, a popular haunt of young professionals, themselves breathing new life into cafés and boutiques and mixing genially with the remnant staid folk of former years. In jeans, a black T-shirt and comfortable old runners, one lace permanently untied, the man sat clutching a postcard graced on its cover by a series of snow-white terraced rock formations, each with a cool blue pool of water highlighting a gorgeous landscape.

He started out conversing in his usual manner, pushing his heavy brown hair back when he raised a question, and then letting his companion dominate the conversation while he sat and thought. "Why would they have taken a bus to the middle of ... where did you say? Cappador?"

"Cappadocia," replied the young woman, flipping through her mobile to research the question.

"Bleedin' 'eck, where's that, our Jenn?"

"It's in the middle of Turkey, Uncle Nige."

"Hmm … *delight*-ful, if you'll pardon the expression … hope there's something there besides goats and carpets." Nigel loved a good play on words and was referring to the storied candy. He took a long draught of his pint of bitter.

"What puzzles me," his niece added, pointing at the postcard, "is there's no cheeky message, just 'Hi from Pamukkale, on our way to Cappadocia' and that's it."

"Pamucklee," he mispronounced and anglicized. "That's those white cliffs. Saw't once on the Beeb."

"Yes, I remember."

"That's weird, though. You're right. Usually, they write a load of cheek."

His brow was knitted, though no one would notice, his hair falling continually over his eyes and forehead, pushed back repeatedly by his free hand, a gentle tic of modesty and a habit long entrenched to deal with life outside the hair in short doses. For his niece, with hair kept longer with Brunhilde plaits and dressed smartly in a summer print, the pub was part of a weekend getaway back north from the behemoth that is London, to catch up with family and to enjoy the pop-culture scene that had come to fascinate her and her video camera over the years. Having drained her half of bitter, she made her way to the bar to order another two, wondering why her sister, with all her wealth, would take a fancy to a field of goats without providing a silly story.

"Any word?" Augustus Krauledat asked.

"None. The bushy-brow Swedish good-for-nothing. Why you send me him, Augustus?" Funar moaned.

"He came recommended Funar. *Scheisse*," he cursed. "Perhaps a little more faith, huh?"

"We'll see, I guess. We'll see." Funar was not happy.

"You've gone very quiet. Missing home again?" Erik asked.

"Yes, I suppose so," Baldwin replied. "My mobile network doesn't work here either. I feel cut off."

"Maybe that's a good thing. Allows you time to think."

"To think … what a concept," Baldwin threw back softly.

Baldwin was driving and, as they were approaching Konya, they saw a strange sight near a filling station — a man doubled over in some considerable distress. An ambulance was parked at the scene and a paramedic was speaking to him. The man kept pushing the attendant away. They drove on. Time was of the essence for their task.

Nigel turned the postcard over in his hands a fourth time, examining it in minute detail. The condensation from his pint on his fingers soaked the corner of the Turkish stamp and it slipped slightly, revealing a strange-looking zigzag mark.

И

"Wonder what this backward N is all about?"

On a whim, he wetted the stamp some more with the intent of removing it, knowing his niece who sent the postcard would know he was an ephemeral philatelist with an old scrapbook of stamps. He took out the thinnest of his house keys and nudged the corner of the stamp a little further, revealing more of the strange lettering. Completing the task with another dab of beer, he was able to slide the rest of the stamp clear away, revealing a tightly handwritten script.

Имаме нужда от помощ

He showed Jenn, who shook her head as she pondered.

"Looks Russian, like those strange bits we get on the upper channels of the telly. Why would she hide it under the stamp?"

They both considered this for a moment, Jenn pulling at her lip, deep in thought.

"She knows I would try to save the stamp for my collection." Uncle Nigel added." The trouble is, I can't Google the message beneath it or anything because I can't make those symbols on my old Nokia phone. We need help. Is there one of those Russki churches around here, you know, with the big onion on it?" Nigel pondered aloud.

"No, there's one in Longsight. Maybe you can call them?"

"And say what? What sound does a backward N make? What am I gonna say about this one with the two Ks back to back?"

"What if you Google 'Russian alphabet'?"

"Hmm, let me try."

The screen came up with optional links, most mentioning Cyrillic letters, one with a nice table, a useful Rosetta Stone that gave the equivalent in Latin letters for each symbol.

Jenn read out the interpretation. "So that backward N thingy is a letter I. The H is an N." She looked up at her uncle and rolled her eyes. "Then it says the Y is a U, and the back-to-back K jobbie makes a *zh* sound."

She kept reading for a few moments in silence, until her uncle, growing impatient, said, "What's it all together then?"

She took a clean beer mat and jotted down the corresponding letters in Latin script:

imame nuzhda ot pomosht

Feeling a bit deflated, they realized that, even if it was in Latin script, they didn't know in what language.

"Try your Googly thingy with that line and see what comes up," Uncle Nigel suggested.

She popped in the letters with her thumbs at lighting speed that had her uncle staring at his own hands like they belonged to a sloth.

The language detected was Bulgarian. She raised her eyebrows in alarm, immediately showing the screen to her uncle.

we need help

They dashed out of the pub to the nearest police station.

The night bus pulled out of Konya with the boys and their mother feeling much calmer than they'd been during their high adventure in the afternoon. They'd taken the Volkswagen to the police station near the centre of Konya. The desk officer was young and out of his element. The senior officer of the precinct, however, spoke reasonable English and listened closely to their story, taking notes and details about the strange dark-haired man with prominent eyebrows and a curious, almost impossible-to-peg accent. The boys broke into giggles when they explained how they subdued the man with Turkish delight and a yo-yo but grew more sombre when the officer lectured them that the man was dangerous, moving cars were even more dangerous, and that they should let police do their work from here forward.

While they waited in the spartan interview room, the senior officer was quickly able to corroborate their story through discussions with their counterparts in Denizli about the hostel manager who was found shaken but largely unharmed, and through a radio message from the ambulance service that they'd attended to an uncooperative man reportedly in distress at a petrol station on the western outskirts. Two officers were dispatched to pick up the man at the hospital where he was taken for a broken nose and swollen genitalia. When questioned regarding motive, the mother said evasively that they assumed the man intended to rob them but that their intervention confounded his plans. She and the boys were released. Sadie took the boys to a nearby café, bought them each a cold drink and said, "Boys, I'm not sure that we should carry on here. I didn't think it would be this dangerous!"

"What?" yelled Romy with tears in his eyes. He was still feeling bad about the keep-away game on the Istanbul terrace. Guy didn't yell. He just sat there with the saddest look on his face imaginable, started sobbing and stammered out, "I don't care about those old coins, but I want Maimuna!"

Sadie contemplated the situation and realized how invested the boys were now in their travelling adventure — comparing with how she'd initially had to convince them both to undertake it. They'd moaned for days about missing their friends at school. Also, she realized that it was the first time she could remember them releasing strong emotions since the death of their kind father, who'd doted on them whenever he could get away from his restaurant.

"Okay," she announced, drying their tears with a tissue she'd pulled form her purse. "We have to be careful, and we have to be brave, and we have to work together with no more secrets," she added, looking at Guy. "But yes, okay, let's go get Maimuna!"

With those vows affirmed verbally by each boy, and Sadie insisted they say them out loud, they caught a coach and were now headed to Nevşehir, anxious about not providing full disclosure to the police of their intentions to complete their quest to retrieve Maimuna the monkey.

Early the following afternoon, Erik and Baldwin stood in a hostel in Göreme, at a former Eastern Orthodox church complete with frescoes of Saint George and Saint Nicholas on the ceiling, amid the landscape of fairy chimneys and pinnacles of Cappadocia carved over the years into the soft volcanic tuff.

"How is it that you're here, so far from your homeland?" Erik asked the Australian tour operator.

"I came seven years ago, like many from Aus, to visit the monument at Gallipoli," she said. "Then went a little further walkabout and ended up here. Fell in love with and married a Turkish fella."

"But you run the operation alone?"

"My man is in jail at the moment," she admitted.

"Oh? Not a serious crime we hope?"

"Oh, *noi*." To the average ear, *no* grew an i in Aussie English. "Nothing serious. He tried to build a step up to our door. But heritage laws are very strict here. He'll be out next month. It was that or we pay a huge fine."

"Okay… I thank you for meeting with us. You recall them then, the family we spoke of?"

"Yeah, mate, great kids. Mom was a good laugh too. We got on right fine. My hired guide took them to Derinkuyu this morning, they should still be there now, unless delayed to this arvo." She was an open book.

"Now, Mom? Now can we go to the carpet place? Now?" Guy asked.

"Yes, it's on our tour. I've told you. We visited the caravanserai this morning, now we'll visit the carpet store coming up in Nevşehir, then we go to the underground city at Derinkuyu. The nice Aussie lady explained it to us. She even sent word to them in advance about our visit. It's coming up no ... and here it is."

The minivan pulled up to a bright-red sign announcing Ozil Kilim in gold letters on a black backing. Colourful kilims hung everywhere, as if displaying to the entire world were necessary to draw in customers. They eagerly dismounted the minivan, not in the least because their driver chain-smoked throughout the tour.

"Now I know where the expression 'smokes like a Turk' comes from," Sadie muttered.

They were eager to meet Ozil and entered the shop.

The nurse at the regional hospital in Konya handed Olof some painkillers and an ice pack; the young doctor had just examined and reset his nose, which was still rather swollen and now covered in a white plaster cast and bandage. In contrast, dark circles were starting to appear under his eyes amid yellowing skin. He stood up, sharp pains stabbing through his swollen groin as he did so. Gritting his teeth, he looked down the hallway and noticed two police officers at the nurses' station. He slowly turned the other way and exited through a fire door, painfully taking the stairs down and leaving the building through a door backing onto the parking area. He found a car parked behind a pillar and, with a calculated jolt, put his elbow through the passenger window, shattering the glass. Unlocking the car, he crawled below the dash, gritting his teeth in pain, started the car and drove off in the direction of Nevşehir.

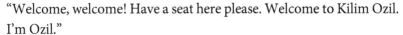

"Welcome, welcome! Have a seat here please. Welcome to Kilim Ozil. I'm Ozil."

The man was in his sixties, a veteran in sales and of understanding the importance of establishing relationships, having inherited the business from his father and grandfather before him. Sadie and the boys sat down on a cushioned bench, the older boy, Romy, spinning a yo-yo.

"So you're from Australia?"

"No, the lady at our accommodation is from Australia."

"Oh, I see." *You all sound the same to me*, he thought, slightly annoyed. "Well, so you have toured the caravanserai, and they explained the function well?"

"Yes, sort of an overnight station for old camel caravans. We found it very interesting — we tried to imagine the stories the walls could tell," Sadie offered.

"Yes, very good. I see you have really tried to embrace your experience here in Turkey."

"You don't know the half of it," Sadie said grinning. They all giggled.

"So, apple tea for all?" Ozil offered.

"Sure," said Sadie. The boys groaned. They'd had their fill of apple tea and carpet salesmen in Istanbul.

Sadie took the initiative. "Thank you for the tea. Actually, we have come to see if you received an unexpected visitor in the past few days. A little red-and-gold stuffed monkey?"

"I don't understand…" he replied.

She proceeded to explain their adventures in Istanbul, culminating in the incident where the monkey fell into the truck with the Ozil name, with the carpets destined for Nevşehir. Once the man heard the story, he was touched and looked up. Sadie could see him going over the information in his head. He pursed his lips.

"The carpets that came in yesterday are on this wall over here."

He proceeded to unfurl carpet after carpet on the floor. During the course of unrolling the fourth, a red-and-gold monkey fell astray, rolling toward the boys' feet. They were over-the-moon happy and yelled in unison, "Maimuna!"

The man glowed, very pleased to see the boys so happy. Sadie bought the carpet the monkey fell from at the exorbitant asking price and had it shipped to the UK for another exorbitant sum. The man was pleased to sell a carpet, whatever it took, monkey business and all.

Erik asked the short squat man at the counter of the Nevşehir bus station if he had seen the two blond boys with a woman. The man explained in his best English that he had not, but that some buses proceed on to Göreme at request of the passengers. An Australian woman getting a coffee at the canteen overheard the conversation and asked, "Can I help you blokes? I have a Sheila and her two young ankle biters staying with me that sound like what you're on about."

Erik was surprised at this stroke of luck and explained to her that he was looking for them, as were the authorities in the UK and Greece, as well as their families.

"Crikey, I wouldn't have thought that … they didn't let on … they'd be out at the underground city at Derinkuyu this time of the afternoon, near the end of their tour. I'd requested they ring at some point for menu planning and they rang me at lunch to say they'd be back for dinner and had a great day already, something about getting their monkey back. I can't wait to see them this evening to get the full story, they're such fun."

He took note of the location and set out with Baldwin for the underground city museum of Derinkuyu.

Olof sat outside the carpet shop. His heart skipped a beat when he saw them come out, taking turns clutching the monkey and posing for photos. They boarded a minivan and set off. He followed four or five car lengths away in the newly stolen Ford Otosan.

The underground city museum at Derinkuyu was a marvel for any traveller. Down multiple levels, visitors could explore numerous chambers formerly carved and occupied by the Hittites, Medes, Assyrians and later by Christians escaping persecution before Emperor Constantine declared Christianity to be the official religion of the Roman Empire.

The boys had great fun running around the tunnels, chasing each other and pretending their own game of modern warfare — to the chagrin of their mother, who was hoping they'd pick up some interest in history, ask the odd question, but to no avail. They were in their own world, and happy to be so. Seeing their resilience after such an awful experience, she chuckled and smiled, sipping through her teeth to strain the grounds of a thick coffee she'd picked up on the way into the museum.

As the boys turned a corner on the second level above the entrance, they received the fright of their life. There, standing in front of them, was the man who still haunted their thoughts nightly, dressed in a filthy green bloodstained shirt, tattered black jacket and dusty Doc Martens.

"All right, boys! Party is over! Give me the monkey! Now!"

In addition to their fear, the boys began to feel something else. Anger. This man — yet again — this man who had frightened them and their mother.

"Here's the monkey, you creep," said Guy.

He held it out to the man, who reached for it instinctively. Instantly, Guy tossed it in the air over his shoulder, gave it a hacky-sack like kick behind his back and over Olof's head. Olof scrambled to reach it, and Romy, seeing his chance, brained him with his yo-yo squarely on the bandage of his broken nose, shattering the plaster cast and the newly mending cartilage. Olof screamed in pain, stumbling backward and tumbling through an opening in the wall to the passage below.

Baldwin and Erik entered the museum complex, looking for the blond boys. About ten minutes into the self-guided tour, near the lower base of the complex, a man fell at their feet from an upper level, unconscious from his fall. From his face and build, notwithstanding a bandage and plaster on his nose, Erik recognized the man from a description given to him from his colleagues in Istanbul. He immediately called the police on his mobile while Baldwin watched over the stranger.

"So, Costos, you can report to Petras that the family is safe," Erik said. "The mother, a Sadie D'Arnaud, told me they're continuing their adventure to the south coast, and from there to Crete. They contacted their UK family to tell them as well."

"And the coins?" Costos pursued.

"They gave them to the Turkish authorities, insisting that they return to a museum instead of a private collection so that people can see them. You can confirm this with MIT."

"Shit! I don't see them getting into a museum in Turkey, nor will they be returned to the Bulgarians, who probably have the best claim. Well … good work. If MIT confirms, as far as we're concerned, you're now released from your obligation. You're free to go."

"Please send me that in writing." He gave the man his email address and turned to Baldwin. "You still up to travel home?"

Baldwin was delighted.

"Why don't we head to Rhodes first on our way?"

"Sure!" Baldwin smiled, his blue eyes sparkling with happiness.

Oncle Etienne's phone rang continually on his desk at the mill while he wheezed his way up the short flight of stairs back from the toilets, having to pause halfway up to catch his breath.

"*Ja*, hallo," he gasped out.

"Where is my money?" barked Augustus on the other end.

"I've had … family complications. Access to some bank accounts, but not others. I … I need help to find my brother and nephew for … for a passcode issue. They're travelling together. Leave it with me a bit longer."

"I've heard all about this brother and his boy. Use the contacts you were given. And don't call me until you have the money!" With that, he hung up the line.

Etienne put his head in his hands, the tears in his eyes obscuring a semi-tame pigeon that had landed on the windowsill of his dusty, old office.

The old Nokia rang its ditty.

"Uncle Nige, have you heard anything?"

"Oh, yes, yes! She phoned! They're all safe!" he replied.

"Thank heavens! That was way to much excitement for this girl. What an adventure! Those boys are having the time of their life travelling about like that. I'm going to wring the full story out of our Sadie when I get a chance."

"Yes, I'm happy too. Imagine running around Turkey with two young boys. She's always had a mind of her own, our Sadie." He shoved the hair out of his eyes, then caught the eye of the barkeep with a raised-glass gesture to bring him another pint. "How's London?" he asked, being polite and wanting to bring some balance to his care and concern for both of his nieces.

"Meh!" Jenn registered boredom in her voice. "I feel like hopping on a plane to Anywhere!"

PART 4

WHERE DREAMS TRAVEL, WHERE TRAVELLERS DREAM

The rain had fallen nonstop for days. A cold low-pressure system clung to the Mediterranean shores, bringing all but the largest and most tested vessels to port. Ferries, lashed with sheets of spray, were wedged alongside the windswept quays until a slight lull in the weather would allow some to service the frustrated travellers stranded ashore.

For three days, Erik and Baldwin sat pensively watching the storm out of a smeared café window in the coastal town of Marmaris, frustrated to see the expenses nibble away at their dwindling supply of currency, the younger man's banking cards inexplicably denied in the local banks. Someone at home had put a hold on his access; he could venture to guess who — a certain uncle coming to mind.

The journey to the coast had not been relaxing. Their rental car had been sabotaged, the break lines cut outside of Antalya. Had Erik not cleverly geared down and used their parking brake to skid clear of an oncoming truck on the slick shoulder — Baldwin shook the thought off and took another sip of coffee. He grimaced thinking of the way they'd finished their journey, cramped in the passenger side of a delivery van making its way to the port with boxes of porcelain tile and cheap electronics. They didn't know why, but once again, it was clear — someone was following them.

"We haven't seen any sign of anyone following us in days," Erik said, breaking the long silence, "and the rain is finally easing. What about taking a Jetfoil over to Rhodes?"

Baldwin practically jumped out of his chair to get his things together. Erik smiled and the two headed out the door of the café.

An hour later, the Jetfoil was unleashed by a lithe, dark-haired woman in uniform and heels tottering with the thick mooring rope on the narrow deck in front of the forward doors. Casting off, the journey quickly deteriorated into a series of rolls threatening to toss them into the lap of Poseidon. Struggling briefly, the uniformed woman deftly popped back inside the boat and began offering coffee to the white-faced passengers. The repetitive bouncing challenged the hearts and minds of all. Again and again, the craft pounded into the oncoming waves; again and again, the two men rolled in their seats or slammed into the bulkhead below the porthole window to their right, their efforts gymnastic as they attempted to balance and avoid spilling the bitter coffees they had just purchased from the dark-haired acrobat in heels.

Finally ashore in Rhodes, they sought shelter, watching all who disembarked behind them for signs of their shadows in pursuit. They saw none, but knew other boats would soon follow.

Four more days passed and the weather remained overcast. The younger man pined for the sun, remembering its brightness, its clarity and how it penetrated to warm his soul during his time on the island of Thasos only a few months earlier. Sunshine, warm sunshine that had brought him out of a long and frustrating stasis and inspired a reinvigorated renewal. A mindset had taken shape of becoming more alive than he'd felt for a very long time. He waited, sometimes patiently, other times in mild frustration. He waited for the sunshine.

"What's with you?" Erik looked curiously at Baldwin, who had a bounce in his step and sense of purpose not seen for days. Enjoying the subtleties of the Greek feel in Rhodes, they'd just finished a relaxing breakfast on a terrace café on a bright but chilly morning overlooking St. Anthony's Gate to the medieval walled city. Their plan for the day was to explore the Palace of the Grand Master of the Knights of St. John.

"I don't know, I just feel better now." He continued to admire the crenellated tower of the palace. He was as happy as if he'd just seen the mighty Colossus reappear in the harbour.

As the weather turned in their favour, they didn't stay much longer in Rhodes. Although they seemed to have lost their tail and enjoyed the island, they were eager to move on when they realized that they were visiting at the wrong time of year for some of the main attractions, including the famous Valley of the Butterflies. It was still early spring and the short days and cool weather lingered.

As if to confirm their decision, Baldwin caught sight of a familiar face in the distance. The man was ordering a coffee near a souvenir stand as he exited a Eurobank lobby. Olof. And with a younger man in dreadlocks and tattered jeans who looked familiar. The two men appeared to be searching together, and Baldwin knew without any doubt it was for him and his father.

Baldwin's mind raced. He was pleased to have been able to finally access some cash after an emergency loan from his Tante Viv. But now there was no time to waste. He would have to deal with his uncle in Belgium later. He walked at a measured pace with Olof in the corner of his eye and doubled back along a narrow street to the ferry terminal where his father waited. They were leaving for Crete in less than an hour. He filled in Erik on his sighting, and upon learning that their pursuers were close, Erik ventured a hunch. He quickly checked the departure board and snatched the carbon paper booking tablet from the counter of the middle-aged attendant. *Who but this old dude still uses these things to book?* he wondered. The attendant was in the midst of writing their tickets and had just stepped away briefly to check a fare for an inquiring tourist who self-importantly butted the queue to ask only one quick question that turned into three or four. Capitalizing on the arrogance, Erik used the pen nib to heavily score the word *Crete*, then tore off the upper white copy. In place of *Crete*, on the white, he substituted Thira in ink, and walked away hurriedly with Baldwin in tow to the quay where the ferry to Thira was just ready to pull up the boarding plank. Safely aboard, they went to the side rail to check for anyone following. Seeing none, they went inside, noticing that the ferry was a little over half full. Baldwin was quiet but compliant.

"What just happened there?" Baldwin asked.

"Hopefully, I've thrown them off our scent."

"Are we still going to Crete? I wanted to see Knossos and the frescoes of Minoan bull jumping … all the stuff I read about while we were stuck in that café for three days in the pouring rain."

"Mmm … no."

"No … no what? Where are we going then?"

"Thira."

"Thira. Where's Thira?"

"Thira is an island northwest of us. It's better known as Santorini, but I used the more obscure name on the ferry ticket to throw off our two shadows in case they double back and ask what other ferries had left about the same time after seeing we're not in Crete. We may still be able to see something Minoan if I have my history right. Did you manage to get some money?"

"Yes, Tante Viv emailed me some cash."

"Emailed you some? I'll have to get you to explain that to me someday. So, while you were at the bank, I was thinking … have you been texting home regularly?"

A blank, non-committal look appeared on Baldwin's face. Resigned to be truthful, he acquiesced, "Yes … why?"

"Who are you texting?"

"Hmm … and how is this your business?"

"Look, I'm not trying to pry. If it's your … special person, that's no concern. But have you been texting Oncle Marcel?"

"Not for a while. He doesn't answer his mobile. Probably busted it with his fat thumbs. He doesn't understand anything electronic. Thinks if you press harder it works better."

"Well then, your Tante Viv?"

"Yes, I send her a note every Saturday."

"Saturday, the day before Sunday."

"Usually."

"And, if we can count on one thing in life, even after all these years, to happen on a Sunday in Damme, what is that?"

"Oncle Marcel and Oncle Etienne sitting in the markt at Café Zonnebloem drinking b — wait ... you don't think?"

"I'm not completely sure, no, but how else have these two on our tail repeatedly found out where we are? For weeks — it's been over two months! We've done everything to cover our tracks, and each time they find us! Konya, our side trip to Antalya, Marmaris, now Rhodes — someone is feeding them information and I suspect that same someone has wheedled away from your aunt and uncle the access to some of your banking information to cut you off. You know how good-natured Marcel and Viv are ... they trust him way too much. And you know that every word you send is relayed to the whole town one waffle at a time."

"Wait — you really think Oncle Etienne has connections to organized crime?"

"Nothing about my miserable older brother would surprise me anymore. Cutting you off like that. It's all to retain control of your money, and because I'm gone, to get you working back in that blasted mill for him to get his pound of flesh out of me through you."

"He must be good at hiding things then. He's really that connected? He never goes anywhere."

"There's one thing I never told you about him yet. It's not a pleasant topic. When I was a young boy, he seemed obsessed as a teenager with the Algemeene-SS Vlaanderen, the Flemish units who signed up voluntarily to fight on the side of Germans in WWII. This was already decades after the war was over, but he would still romanticize about this stuff with a couple of his friends, and some of those friends had friends who later became linked to all sorts of nasty activities in the underworld. One in particular, an ex-Hitlerjugend called Augustus, is quite renowned in the crime circuit. Mean-looking guy, I only saw him once — wears an old suit and evidently lives on beer and sausages."

"How do you know all this? About this guy Augustus, I mean?"

"I used to listen to your uncle's discussions on the phone at the mill. After a while I never trusted Etienne with anything. And one day he asked me to drive to Leipzig to deliver an envelope to a 'supplier.' Strange place for a drop-off — an old ramshackle hunting lodge outside of town. When we arrived, I was told to wait in the truck, and this guy Augustus came out from the doorway and took the envelope. I thought it strange he would live in a place like that, wearing a rumpled old suit. Must also be skinflint cheap, a natural pal for Etienne. Anyway, after that drop-off, Etienne seemed to have all sorts of contacts to take care of the most bizarre requests. Imports of machine parts, equipment, cheap cleaning supplies. Always stuff for the mill that I knew we could have sourced locally. All deliveries would happen at night and he would never involve me, so I think he was importing hot parts and materials, but I left before gathering any proof."

"So you think he has people chasing us to do what? Scare us?"

"I don't know. The Swede, or half-Swede, whatever the hell he is, we know to be dangerous from the monkey adventure. He must have busted out of custody. You say the other guy had dreadlocks?"

"Yes, slim swarthy guy, and I think I remember where I saw him before … it was him and a skinny woman who were dragged out of the sultan's market in Istanbul around the time that the monkey kids got the coins, so somehow they've linked up."

"I've a hunch it was through Funar Grigorescu, the Romanian I was telling you about who smuggles antiquities. I'm told he was a crime kingpin in Cernavodă before moving on to Istanbul, on the lam from the Romanian authorities. He's known to be linked with Augustus, but again, it's just a hunch. In the meantime, we're away again, at least for now, and I'm hoping those two comb the ferry terminal, ask questions, and through the ticket pad think we've gone to Crete. That should buy us a few days anyway."

"Hope so. I want to see something of the Minoans."

"You have interesting priorities."

"Well, if I wanted to just run away all the time, I might as well just fly back to Belgium."

"Okay, I understand. I warned you at one point about travelling with me."

"And I'm just fine with it. As it stands now though, maybe I should warn you about travelling with me!"

The ferry docked at the landing point of Athinios in Santorini. Baldwin disembarked and was immediately struck by the dramatic upsweep of the inner slope, which kissed the cloudless sky high above. At the jagged ridge along the top, the sun was in his eyes and he could barely make out the crest. Fifteen minutes later, in a large minibus, they climbed in long slow sweeps the series of switchbacks taking them far above the sea. Baldwin glanced below to see the surf lapping against the narrow shore, then looked up again just as the vehicle crested the top of the final rise, this time with the sun over his right shoulder. The scene before him took his breath away; the island's upper rim presented a riot of bright whitewashed buildings, interconnected and hugging the steep upper slopes in a myriad arrangement, with windows largely shuttered and topped with striking powder-blue domes: a Greek-postcard scene that continually unfolded before his eyes as the bus progressed toward the centre of the town of Fira.

Erik explained from a brochure that the steeply sloped island was really the remnant of an ancient volcano that had exploded around 2500 BC, leaving the semicircle rim of a caldera. The  effect of having three-hundred-metre steep slopes on both sides was not lost on Baldwin; it was one of the most strikingly beautiful scenes he'd ever experienced, notwithstanding the commercialization that had evidently overtaken the island in recent years.

"So, you mentioned Minoans?"

Erik smiled and shook his head. "Can we at least find somewhere to stay first and get some sleep?"

"Oh yeah … sorry … I forgot. First things first. I'm hungry anyway."

In Rhodes, Dreadlocks began to interview the thirty-something attendant at the ferry terminal's tourist information desk. She looked part Romani, which appealed to him in some way he couldn't define; maybe the heavy eyebrows? Shaking these distractions away, he pulled out photos of Erik and Baldwin, taken boarding a Jetfoil in Marmaris. *They'd been that close!* The attendant looked at Baldwin's photo and shook her head, then at Erik's and one of those alluring eyebrows rose. She gestured toward the ticketing agent's counter and the middle-aged man who attended. The man nodded at Erik's picture then sat staring. A twenty-euro note was produced, which seemed to loosen things up, for the man thumbed his way through the yellow carbon copies on his desk and produced the one linked to Erik's purchase: Heraklion, Crete. Keeping the form close to his chest, the man made to hand the carbon copy over, but then pulled it back and nodded slightly toward the information attendant. Twenty more euros were produced.

Dreadlocks looked over the copy, nodded at the man and hurried out to the Yiannis Tavérna to pass on what he learned to his new boss, the half-Swedish brute with a severely misshapen nose and a tongue still beet red and permanently damaged. He didn't have the courage yet to ask him how it happened. Based on his strength, it must have been someone huge and powerful. He was just pleased not to have been killed in Turkey, and after waking up on a park bench with his girlfriend, he had her crash in a small apartment near the antiquities shop in Istanbul, offered by his boss, until he could raise enough funds to move them somewhere else. It was not ideal, close to the miserable

Romanian proprietor. She often reminded him that she missed her sister in Cadiz. Still, she also added in rebellion, that anything was better than life with her parents, despite the crappy local coffee.

Etienne sat at his kitchen table smoking like he had most Wednesday nights for the previous ten years. Wednesday night was delivery night, just before midnight at the mill, and he found smoking was the only way to keep him awake until the truck arrived from Pristina. He hated the Kosovar driver, always insisting on some euros on the side just to keep his stinking garlic mouth shut. In his mind, no one in the area could understand his silly Albanian babble anyway, but Etienne didn't want to take any chances. Even after all these years, he still didn't completely trust his arrangement with that lout Augustus, a man he feared tremendously but suffered in silence because he wanted no one to know of his secret dealings. He chewed on the end of his hand-rolled cigarette and thought of the past Sunday when he learned his youngest brother and nephew were headed for Rhodes, cursing that his information supply was limited to weekly updates from his tired old sister-in-law. Then there was the disgusting task of phoning at exorbitant expense the greedy Romanian to relay information to a useless half-caste Swede and his Dago sidekick to keep them on the trail. *What a life*, he thought. He went to light up another but dozed off in his chair. His mind wandered, a troubled expression pinching his face as his eyes remained heavy.

> *Mesdames et messieurs, voici M. Van Ryssel, qui est accusé de collaboration avec les unités allemandes pendant la deuxième guerre mondial.*

Etienne was horrified. *Why are they accusing me of collaboration with German units during the Second World War?*

The tribunal was made up of a Tunisian, another even darker man — Congolese by appearance — and another, obviously Walloon based on the rooster logo he'd pinned to his cardigan, all speaking French, and a common representation of the French-speaking regions of Belgium. Here he was in his own country being judged by three foreigners who had no business even stepping foot in Flanders!

En plus, il est accusé d'avoir encouragé un état d'esclavage dans son moulin dans la banlieue du village de Damme autour de Bruges.

This is preposterous! I've never kept any slaves at my mill, and it's Brugge dammit, a Flemish city, niet in de strontzak frans!

Finalement il est accusé d'avoir volé les fonds bancaires de son neveu afin d'arranger ses affaires farfelues, pour sa vie qui sera très courte dès que maintenant.

What do they mean I'm accused of having stolen from my nephew's bank account for illicit business? What do they mean my life from here will be short?

He woke up suddenly, coughing, gasping and wheezing, his emphysema threatening to take his life. He was in a cold sweat and shaking. He stumbled to the sink to sip some water, and then the short distance to the door outside. He flung it open to take the biggest breath his damaged lungs would allow. To his surprise and horror, there stood his brother Marcel with a severe-looking older man in a rumpled suit. Augustus.

Etienne's eyes grew large, and he lost his balance and fainted, falling forward flat on his face on the flagstones of his front walk.

"Focking fabulous," Augustus remarked.

In the morning sun of Santorini, Erik and Baldwin packed a lunch and took a rattletrap Mercedes taxi that had seen one too many tourist seasons to the village of Pyrgos, and then set out on foot up the eight-hundred-metre rise that makes up Mount Profitis Ilias. The scenic upland offered a full view of the island, including the monastery at its peak, as well as the archaeological dig of Akrotiri in the distance.

"So, up we go," Baldwin said, looking at a free, poorly designed tourist map crowded on the edges with advertisements of hotels, hostels and seafood restaurants.

"Looks like a good climb and the weather looks to be fine. Going to keep my eye on those patchy clouds though," Erik cautioned.

Over their heads, huge bright-white clouds were moving through in droves, pushed by a strong upper wind that made them travel quickly across the sky. Those on the land below found themselves alternating between a flood of sunlight and dismal shadow, each for minutes at a time. During their long steady climb, Erik pondered the scale of the ancient volcanic explosion that obliterated almost all traces of the ancient Minoans and any others living on the island at the time. Some said that the lands subsiding were the basis of the legend of Atlantis. In his reverie, he hiked up the trail, looking in the distance, and promptly tripped and fell over Baldwin who had stopped without warning to squat down with his pack.

"What are you doing? You don't just stop without warning me!" Erik stretched his leg after getting up, happy to have avoided twisting his knees.

"You were right behind me. Can't you see when I stop?" Baldwin looked bemused by his father's tumble.

"Yes, unless I'm trying to make out something, and with the light going up and down like this, I can't always see ... I mean, I don't always want to be looking down." He arched his back with a sigh, then stared for a moment into the distance. "Do you see that area where they've been digging over there?"

Baldwin squinted initially but then focused on the scene of an archaeological dig in the distance. He took a drink from his water bottle as he examined the scene and, after swallowing, he nodded. "Yes."

"That's Akrotiri, what's left of a settlement of Minoans after a great volcanic explosion around 2500 BC."

"So, let me get this straight. We miss out on the Temple of Knossos and the bull jumpers in Crete to look at a few holes in the ground? Are you serious?"

"Look, I had to get us out of there. I'm sorry that Crete was off the list. By the way, what was so important that you had to stop?"

"I got a text."

"So what?" Erik said, shaking his head a couple wags with a bemused look.

"So it's been a while, and I wanted to see who sent me something."

"You're hiking up a slope in one of the world's beauty spots … and you … want to answer a text?"

"Yeah, and let's just say it wasn't Tante Viv."

Erik sighed. "Okay, as long as we're careful who we tell where we are until we get rid of our little problem."

"Understood… Oh, sorry … that's why you want to know, isn't it. You okay?"

"Yes, the only thing hurt from my spill was my feelings." Erik chuckled. "Let's continue on."

At a good pace, they hiked to the top of the mountain and circled the peak near the monastery of Profitis Ilias, shaking their heads now and then at human interventions that spoiled the views in some directions with radar antennae and a rusted communications tower, while the wide open vistas in other directions were breathtaking. Together with the fresh spring breeze in their faces, the deep-blue colour of the sea, the reddish-black hues of the cliffs, and on this occasion, the smoke emanating from the crater of Nea Kameni, the panorama of natural beauty brought tears of joy to their eyes. They'd found another spot to consider their own, as father and son, and Santorini was turning out to be well worth the detour.

Olof was furious. *I need that kid's bank password or there'll be no more work for the Romanian, and I'm skint!* He'd been bullying the dreadlocked Spaniard to cover most of their expenses. They'd only just missed the two Belgians for the second port in a row, and now they were on the red-eye ferry to Crete, together with a class of teenagers on term break who kept them up deep into the night as they did their best to sleep in the lounge. There was no sleep to be had as the teens laughed their way throughout the whole night. As silence finally reigned approaching dawn, he exacted his revenge. Finding in a utility compartment an aerosol air horn, he let blast into the huddled mass of dozing kids and petrified them. As they screamed in a panic — a couple wet their pants — he laughed hysterically, one of the most evil-sounding laughs one could ever generate. A ship's mate approached as the horn finally exhausted its contents and looked to engage Olof in a strong dressing down for disturbing the peace. He took one look at Olof's disfigured face and decided a calm warning was sufficient despite the screaming protests of the teenagers when it became clear he was not going to be incarcerated. Fabian looked on in quiet amusement. During their short time together, usually it was him on the end of Olof's vicious streak.

"You're behind on payments!" Augustus was matter of fact. There was no greeting, no nonsense as he burst through the door and sat at Etienne's small kitchen table. Marcel had just finished picking up Etienne from his front walk and reluctantly half carried, half dragged him and set him down in an armchair in the corner, propping him up with a small pillow against the wall at his back. There were lace doilies on the arms of the chair, pinned there and prickling his arm, gifts from Viv. *Just to taunt me*, he thought.

Still very pale, his hands shaking, Etienne collected his thoughts and wheezed out a sentence. "Yes, I know … I'm trying to get the money to you."

Marcel was not impressed. He had been at home exhausted after a long day of work at the dockyards in Knokke and sitting in his own comfortable chair, minus the doilies that he'd ripped off years ago to Viv's chagrin. A pintje of Jupiler in hand, he'd been watching the Anderlecht vs. Antwerp football match he'd had Viv record for him when the strange old fellow in a suit had pounded on his door and asked for Etienne. Marcel hadn't recognized the face, and as was his manner, he asked how he knew Etienne.

"Through Decroos ... Victor."

Marcel recognized the name as the brother of one of Etienne's companions in school. Trusting as he was, he saw no reason to not do as the man asked and escorted him to his brother's cottage.

Now his brother was in the hot seat. Marcel had given him a pack of frozen peas wrapped in a tea towel to put on the rising lump on his forehead, almost dwarfing in size the neighbouring wart. Evidently he owed the stranger a substantial amount of money.

"I can't accept promises. I need the money now!" Augustus insisted.

Marcel, seeing his brother in a worrisome state, asked the natural question. "How much does he owe you, and for what?"

"I've had my people supplying him with spare parts for the mill for years. He owes me fifteen thousand euros, and I want it now."

Marcel thought for a moment and went beet red in the face. Then, seeing that it wouldn't be to his advantage to blow up in front of the man from Germany, he saved his wrath for the brief interval when Augustus left to use Etienne's toilet.

Is he too cheap to pay to piss at a petrol station? Marcel wondered, before he turned to his brother and said in an aggressive but quiet whisper, "So let me guess, this is why you wanted Baldwin's main account blocked? So he can't access it during his trip? You know he has not only what he's earned in there from working, but also his mother's life insurance funds, don't you? Can you imagine what someone would have to put him through for him to give up the codes? Force him to go to a bank to withdraw under threat of punishment? Just because you want to use the money! *Mô*, you are such an asshole sometimes! How dare you! And now you're pulling us down with a gangland loan of fifteen thousand euros? How do you live with yourself?"

There was no answer. Etienne slumped forward in his chair and was nonresponsive to the questions, still struggling weakly for breath. Alarmed, Marcel helped his brother to his narrow bed in the back bedroom of the cottage and opened his shirt around the collar, then rushed out into the kitchen, picked up the phone and called an ambulance.

Augustus emerged from Etienne's small bathroom, popping the rickety bifold door off its track in his haste, and looked around quickly.

"What has happened? Where is he?"

"You have him wrapped in knots. He's having trouble breathing. I've called an ambulance."

"I must have that money! He told me once he had access to more funds in another account."

"Then you may be out of luck. He doesn't have the password to our nephew's acc—"

Marcel realized before this last statement was fully out of his mouth how badly he might have screwed up, and how he'd possibly put Baldwin in danger. He had no idea what information Augustus had already wheedled out of Etienne, but nevertheless, he cursed his own stupidity.

Erik was lying on the bench by the picture window in the front room of their accommodation, his preferred spot over the swayed mattress on the single bed he'd endured their first night in Fira. He was trying to make sense of their situation with the two men in pursuit when exhaustion overcame him from the long walk he'd taken with Baldwin up the slope of Mount Profitis Ilias. Nodding off, he drifted into a vivid dream.

The towpath along the canal through the polders left no history on file. No one knew who dug the original canal and no one knew when the well-worn paths on either side were first formed. In his vision, he saw hunched-over peasants digging. He was riding the bicycle furiously, his eye across the canal, where a woman rode vigorously in parallel, the one from Namur who was his delight in life, the one who now had a determined look on her face that he couldn't read…

In the distance, workmen were getting ready to raise the bridge. He had maybe less than five minutes to get over to the other side. If the bridge was raised, it would be another twenty kilometres of riding to join her ... he pedalled furiously...

Another two minutes and he would make it ... he glanced over to the other side just as he approached the bridge ... she was gone!

He woke up feeling devastated and swore. His wife had passed away many years ago, and he'd never gotten over the fact that he wouldn't see her again, with so many thoughts unexpressed, especially the true explanation as to why he'd left her and their young son. He dearly hoped that they'd meet again in the afterlife. He went for a walk to clear his mind in the grey predawn light.

Etienne was in the hospital in Bruges in intensive care, struggling for every breath. His tongue swollen, it was not a pretty sight. Marcel and Vivienne sat by his side, watching the life slowly escape with each laborious breath, saddened to see how life had turned out for him. Even to this point, even when they knew how misguided his views were, how his bigotry, his devious plots to control and his resentfulness had damaged their family over the years, they still chose to see him as a brother, as family.

By morning he was gone.

They'd combed Heraklion for a full day when Olof took a phone call on his mobile, made two other calls, and received one back again. He returned to Dreadlocks, who was looking at a rack of postcards of voluptuous nudes. Seeing Olof approach, he turned to him, bracing for the bad news, or worse, another punch in the head.

There was fury in Olof's voice. "They're not here in Crete!"

"Where are they then?"

"They took the ferry two days ago to Santorini!"

Dreadlocks looked blank. "How do you know?"

"The ferry company had a puzzling situation where the ship's manifest had two passengers that didn't show up despite purchasing tickets for Crete, and meanwhile two extra passengers were on the ferry to Athinios in Santorini with the same ticket numbers."

Dreadlocks shrugged. "Well, I saw a copy of their tickets. They said Crete—"

"What copy of the ticket did you see?"

"The second one, the yellow copy."

"And you did not think to question the ticketing representative at the ferry boarding point?"

"No ... I was already forty euros in bribes into it and thought we had the right trail."

He didn't see it coming, a quick left hook to his cheek that left him staggering back in pain.

"You screw up one more time and I won't be as lenient as I was in Istanbul. You'll be at the bottom of the Aegean!"

Marcel was walking to his car to fetch an umbrella for Viv. They were just leaving the funeral service at the Our Lady of the Ascension Church in Damme when it had started to rain, and they still had the cemetery service to attend.

Augustus emerged from a café door. "I must have that money!" he shouted tersely.

Marcel walked up to him and stopped, face looking down at the older man, nose to nose, water dripping down their cheeks.

"Leave this town, and leave my family alone. My wife and I don't have that kind of money, and even if we did, you'd be the last to see it. The mill business will be tied up in probate for years. Now kindly fuck off outta here!"

Augustus scowled at the rotund figure of Marcel and walked away. He pulled out his mobile and made calls to Victor Decroos at the Zeebrugge dockyard and to the Romanian in Istanbul.

Baldwin and Erik had arrived at Piraeus in the morning and were on the short commuter train to Athens. Baldwin, who had marvelled at the scenery in Santorini, now compared it with the grey drudgery of the gateway to this large city. It was with some amusement that he glanced up to see in the neighbouring car the mother and two blond boys he'd first noticed in Sofia, and who had dealt a severe blow a while back, in Cappadocia, to one of the men who pursued them. Erik had dozed off and he didn't want to disturb him to point them out, nor did he care to disturb the family as he was not in the mood for small talk. Similarly, the woman looked to be staring out at the featureless string of buildings going by, the boys asleep on either side, leaning on her. Perhaps their ferry ride from wherever they'd been in the interim was as bumpy as their own. *Quite the grand tour for the lucky little buggers*, he thought. Turning to Erik again, who had just woken, he was ready to voice that he hoped the Acropolis visit was worth it, but thought better of it, shaking the thought from his head. He would regret it later if he gave it short shrift just because he was a bit tired this morning.

Erik and Baldwin disembarked and promptly checked in to a budget hostel before they set out into the streets to get a flavour of life in the Greek capital. It didn't take long for first impressions to form, as a throng of protesters speaking out against financial austerity measures filled Syntagma Square around them. They looked in the distance across the square and saw the line of riot police on foot with tall Plexiglas shields and batons, and behind them, others in helmets mounted on horses. They faced the angry mob who were shaking placards deriding the International Monetary Fund, the European Union and local government figures, whose poster-sized portraits were scrawled with grafitti.

Erik motioned to Baldwin to slip away with him, and they retreated from the scene, not wanting any part in the violent struggle that was likely to follow. Within a half hour they'd ascended the Acropolis to the strings of a cello drifting up from the Odeon of Herodes Atticus. They enjoyed the more relaxed atmosphere atop the city, taking photos of the caryatids and the Parthenon, picturing in their minds the intellectuals in ancient times engaged in debates on the great stone steps of the buildings in one of the crucibles of Western thought.

After their descent, they were enjoying an iced coffee when Baldwin received a text from his Tante Viv: *Slecht nieuws. Uw Oncle Etienne overleed in het ziekenhuis. Begrafenis was vandaag. Laat het uw reis niet verstoren.* Baldwin was shocked. Oncle Etienne had died in the hospital, and his funeral already happened! *Mô.*

Baldwin was annoyed but understood why Tante Viv didn't want it to interfere with his trip. Though he didn't always see eye to eye with the man, he certainly didn't wish death to overtake him. He showed Erik the text, who in turn slumped in his café chair, staring into the distance in disbelief and thinking of all of the ramifications for their family.

Erik soon became distraught, moved to tears. He half cursed, half mourned his older brother's death within the same thought. Theirs had never been a warm relationship. He wondered what it would have been like to have all brothers getting along, all on the same page of family caring.

Erik had heard of others who had lost siblings too early and the profound effect it had on their mentality, how it woke them up to breathe new life into every day as they confronted their own mortality. He had heard how their thoughts and feelings were expressed less filtered, more genuine, and how they'd reached out to all they cared about with the possibility, in the back of their mind, that it might be the last time they did anything before life threw them another unexpected twist. In this, they started life afresh, yet relapsed occasionally into a deep grief for having lost one of their own. These alternating mood swings, from high highs to low lows, were part of the process of grieving, and he was about to experience it head-on while travelling with his son. Should he go back to Flanders? It seemed cold and after the fact, since the funeral was already over. Why had Marcel and Vivienne notified them only when it was over? Had they discovered something about him they didn't want to share? Were they perhaps protecting Baldwin from fallout from Etienne's shady business arrangements? He needed time to think and Athens wasn't the place for that. Missing the outdoors, they booked passage on a train northward leaving the next morning. As if to validate their timing, a siren wailed in the background.

It was time to leave Athens, and Erik's raw emotions unfurled as he hugged his son closely outside the ticket office. "Son, it's going to take me some time to get through this, what just happened. But if I have any advice to give at this time, it's this: Don't waste time with those that only take energy from you. Seek out those that give energy, and especially those that share energy back and forth with you."

The ferry attendant couldn't help but notice the disfigured, dark-haired man in Doc Martens, and the smaller fellow with dreadlocks and a swollen eye that looked a rainbow of painful colours as they sat in the lounge of the ferry to Athens. They were drinking bottles of Fix Hellas beer and staring out the window, as if neither wanted to be with the other. After glancing down at a text message, the disfigured man finally said to the other, "We're being pressed even more to capture the younger one for questioning, for his account PIN. Now not just by the old Belgian, but also by the old man in Germany."

"And what are we to do with the father?"

"It doesn't matter. We can just take him out."

Dreadlocks shook his head. He knew the latter job might be easier than the former, and it disgusted him that he caught himself thinking this way. They prepared to disembark.

The "express" train was crowded and rumbled along through the northern suburbs of Athens and along the lowlands nestled in the rocky terrain of Thessaly. Opposite and facing Baldwin sat an older man with receding blond hair and a distinguished demeanour, sitting up tall and wearing a suit. His wife was also tall, but Turkic in appearance, with heavy black eyebrows, piercing eyes, a full mouth with even white teeth and smooth olive skin. She wore an elegant dress with intricate embroidery and gold leaf intertwined in the cuffs of her sleeves. Beside Baldwin, next to the window, sat a short girl with big hair and a pretty face with a hint of rosacea on her cheeks, a source of some self-consciousness evidently by the way she let her hair hang over them. She wore a fleece vest with backpacker-chic ripped jeans. This visual, with some allure, was ruined when she spoke, which turned out to be incessantly and with an accent and disturbingly insensitive commentary that spoke chapters of information within the first half hour of the journey.

"Look at all the half-finished houses. These Greeks are lazy!"

"Hmm … they can hear you speak like this, you know," Baldwin said in a low voice.

"These folks? They probably don't know any English."

The older couple sitting across raised their eyebrows. Baldwin noticed and said under his breath, "You shouldn't assume that … most of the young do, so you might want to be careful—"

"Yeah, like, whatevverrrr!" She turned to fully face him. "You have an accent. German is it?"

"Flemish."

"*Phlegm*ish? Like hawking and spitting? So, like, where's that … that … *Phlegm*land place?"

"Flemish is a dialect of Nederlands … what you call Dutch, and it's spoken in Flanders, in Belgium."

"Ohhhh, so it's not the spit, sorry. I thought, like, that sounded strange. Can you tell where I'm from?"

"I'd say New York from your accent."

"Brooklyn. Good one! Wow."

The man across piped up in a refined Scandinavian accent, unable to contain himself any further, "Just curious, young lady, do you know who first settled New York?"

"The Italians?"

"No, the Dutch. It was called New Amsterdam. And you have many Dutch names in New York," he added, looking at Baldwin.

Baldwin nodded. "Yes, Haarlem, Staten, Yonkers … all place names from the Low Countries."

Undeterred, she countered with her own take on her home city. "Well, now that I think about it, I thought the English settled it, you know like, the Vanderbilts and the Roosevelts."

"Well, those names sound very English," Baldwin said deadpan with eyebrows raised.

"You got it!"

The irony and sarcasm were not lost on the elder two, both stifling a knowing smile. Glancing briefly at Erik across the aisle, the older man said to Baldwin, "You sound like a wise young man, Fleming. Your father must be proud."

His wife nodded and muttered sadly, "We, too, had a son, a little older than you."

She glanced briefly at her husband who sat stiffly, with a wistful look on his face, and continued in guttural, accented English, "He was always quick to refute stereotypes." She sighed. "He loved to argue and challenge a little too much."

Baldwin didn't like to pry, so he avoided asking the question foremost on his mind about what may have happened to such a fine son.

Vivienne had prepared a post-funeral lunch for the close family and friends at their home. This involved Baldwin's friend Remi and his girlfriend, Yvonne. Once the fresh loaves, ham and pâtés were served along with beer and small glasses of port, the makeshift wake grew a little louder as people opened up, the solemnities over.

Remi inquired to Baldwin's Oncle Marcel, "Any word from Baldwin? I heard he found his father in Bulgaria? That's really something!"

"Yes, he did, and he's very happy. Sends Viv a text every weekend to let her know where he is. He was last in Turkey or Greece or somewhere over there." He looked around the room. "Viv!" he hollered over the din. "Where was Baldwin last?"

"He was on that island with the big statue … you know the one," she hollered back.

"No, I don't know the one. That's why I'm asking."

"It had the big statue in the old times, one of the Seven Wonders, you know. He had a small sketch he made of it in school … used to keep it on his dresser, then he put it away up here somewhere."

Vivienne opened the cupboard above the refrigerator and started rifling through all manner of plastic containers and biscuit tins in search of the precious relic.

"Rhodos," said Yvonne, finally, impatiently.

Remi looked at her with a strange look.

She shrugged. "I'm just guessing by the way Vivienne described it: The Colossus of Rhodes."

"That's it!" shouted Vivienne, more for Marcel's sake than anyone else as she slammed the cupboard door, narrowly missing the ear of a neighbour standing too close. "I told you I knew where he was!"

Remi didn't ask any more questions. He looked sullenly at Yvonne. *How did she know he was in Rhodes?* He downed his pintje of Jupiler beer and went outside, making his way to Etienne's cottage behind the church.

Shortly thereafter, Yvonne thanked and hugged Vivienne and Marcel and went out for a walk along the canal. She needed fresh air. She needed sunshine.

Olof had rounded a corner to the parkade and stolen a Renault Clio within ten minutes of their landing in Piraeus. He was tired of ferries and mass transport and wanted the freedom to rip around, which he did with some vigour on the narrow Athens streets. Dreadlocks's head bumped slightly into the passenger window, further aggravating the headache he'd sustained from his partner's violent outburst the day before. He was texting his girl, who continued to be stuck in the small Istanbul flat until he could send her enough money for them both to leave. *My partner is a psycho. We hope to do this shit soon.*

She replied, almost instantly. *Be careful!*

He slipped his mobile into his denim vest pocket and ventured a question, dreading the response. "So, what do we do now?"

Olof didn't even look at him. He just parked the car, ran into a shop and bought a loaf of bread, a container of hummus and a bottle of water. Back in the car, he ripped off some of the bread, scooped a generous portion of hummus using the crust and stuffed it into his mouth. Once air was allowed in from the chewing, he said, "Funar's contact in Athens saw them climb aboard a northbound train. We head north."

"Where would they go?"

"Playing a hunch … probably Meteora." At his partner's blank look, Olof said, "Meteora. Jesus. Do you know anything? It has the monasteries, it's built on natural rock pinnacles." He turned away, shaking his head. "Quite dramatic."

"Why would they go there?"

"Because, you idiot, if you haven't noticed, wherever they go, they seek out places to hike around and look at nature. If I were them, that's where I'd go."

"You sure they're not headed back to Istanbul?"

"Yes, I am, because the young guy is on his own version of the Grand Tour. They'll head to Italy next unless we find them and sort them out. We don't have much time — the boss is threatening to send someone else after them unless we deliver, pronto. Hey, that's Spanish isn't it? Pronto."

"*Si* … but not the same mean — um, yes, Spanish."

Erik and Baldwin helped the elderly couple who'd sat across from them with their luggage as they descended the train in Kalabaka in the north of Thessaly.

A tout from a budget hotel approached them straightaway, looking Greek but sounding Australian. "You blokes looking to stay in town?"

"Yes," Erik answered. "You sound like you've travelled."

"My mum was born in Brisbane. I can get ya all booked in this arvo if you want. Then you can relax and enjoy some of the nice tucker on offer. We just had Easter so the grilled lamb is still on the go."

"Thank you, we may take you up on that."

Escorting the elderly couple to the Ameliana Hotel, they then followed Aussie boy to the Tavérna Zestós Foúrnos, a family-run bed and breakfast. Seeing the Brooklyn Dodger already tucking into her lunch in the dining room, chatting animatedly with the UK mother and two blond boys, they were tempted to go elsewhere, but exhaustion from the long train ride overtook them and they checked in. Baldwin shook his head. The mom and boys again. *How?*

In a budget hotel in Larissa, where the main highway to the north of Greece dried up to a smaller road, Dreadlocks fell into a deep sleep. He had downed three shots of ouzo to mask the discomfort he felt around Olof and pulled the thin sheet over his head to escape. Soon drifting off, he had a vision…

> His mother, of Moorish descent, struggling with a basket of laundry she carried from the sink to the clothesline she'd strung to the hook near the window of her long-time friend across the narrow calle between the buildings. She was elderly and frail, yet stubbornly hung on to look after him and his older brothers. There was no sign of father. Why did he have to die so young?
>
> *You say he died from grief, Mama? Was he always drunk and gambling, Mama? Why were my father and grandfather taken away early in the morning, dragged out, never to be seen again, Mama? Can you get more money from your family in Córdoba?*
>
> The scene turned ugly in his head, his mother talking to him over the kitchen table. "Fabian, how is it you left me here with your two older brothers, not a wife or even a girl between them? It makes me so sad, and you off over there in the east, doing whatever with that strumpet you call a fiancée. Thankfully you have no money for marriage. She no good for you. You deserve a nice girl."

He saw his brothers come into the flat, the younger of the two, evidently drunk, pulled twenty euros from the ceramic jar on a small shelf above the sink and stuffed it into his shirt pocket. Fabian turned to protest. This was money to help pay the rent, but he froze in shame when he saw the surly look on his brother's face, challenging him to what would turn out to be another beating, his mother crying in grief. All thoughts of championing his mother's cause were buried instantly in his own self-loathing.

He awoke and wept silently. His father's habits had passed to his sons.

Pink roses had been planted against the stone wall on the monastery terrace. Erik and Baldwin had ascended Grand Meteora and were enjoying their view as a giggling young boy threw leaves over the wrought-iron rail. Some of the leaves were caught in the draft and floated upward before eventually descending toward the base of the cliff and to the town below in a slight haze. The vista was spectacular, with sandstone pinnacles eroded over time by the winds and rain to provide a delight of rounded towers, a large natural chessboard complete with crowned pieces spread out in the near distance, challenging invaders since ancient times to hold the Greeks in check. They walked along the rail, away from a newly arrived family.

"Thanks for bringing me here, Papa. This is so beautiful. Reminiscent of Melnik, no?"

"Just what I was thinking, and you're very welcome. Actually, it was me who needed to come here after the news we received and all that bother with the crowds in Athens. Some peaceful time in a monastery might do us some good."

Olof sat in the Renault and started to doze off behind the wheel. It was 4:00 am and he'd come out to the car an hour earlier. He couldn't stand the stifling lack of ventilation in the Larissa pension he'd booked for the night with the young Spaniard. He was also angry with himself for hitting him. Had he not made any mistakes those first weeks on jobs in Berlin?

He thought back to a time when he was that young. He remembered the last conversation he'd ever had with his father, right after he'd completed his last exam in Heidelberg and phoned home to wish his mother a happy birthday. His father had picked up the phone, answering gruffly.

"Your mother is out now, unfortunately. I am busy planning for a three-year diplomatic posting in Greece in two months. How did the testing go? It was Modern European History today, no?"

"No, Modern Asian History ... you know, your blind spot."

"Olof, please don't start ... so, let me guess, you covered British India, the Russian Empire, the Great Game?"

"Yes, the rape of India by the Brits, Russian dominance of the Central Asian vassal states, how people suffered in the crossfire."

"You didn't write that in your answers, did you? Your marks will suffer for such extreme views! We don't pay for you to squander your education—"

"Goodbye Father."

Olof had hung up the pay phone in the corridor of the Heidelberg beer hall and joined a classmate for a large *maas* of the heady amber...

In the Renault, Olof's eyes closed and his chin sunk to his chest...

The beer hall disintegrated, became an empty warehouse where he was tested as a gang member, pressured into beating up a stranger with a bag over his head ... the bag slipped and he saw his father's face ... the warehouse became the basement of a bank where he held a heavily sweating bank manager at gunpoint while the man emptied the contents of the open vault into a leather bag. In a strange, twisted, *Run Lola Run* kind of way, he was next hurtling down the street, then to a waiting black sedan, then in the Tempelhof terminal, then in an underground tunnel. He was running after a child, he was running for a red stuffed monkey, and in a flash, he was punched, kicked and fell backward into open space … falling … falling…

His slipped forward, his head hitting the steering wheel and blowing the horn loudly, causing him to wet himself from the shock.

"So, Mom, what is this place?" Guy asked.

Sadie smiled down at him. "It's a monastery, where monks come to live and pray, like I told you on the ferry."

"Are we staying here all week?"

"No, only for two or three days, like I told you on the ferry."

"Will we see James Bond?" Romy asked.

"No, but we'll see where they made part of his movie when he rides in the gondola basket between two of these tall peaks."

"Which movie?"

"*For Your Eyes Only*, like—"

"I know, I know, like you told us on the ferry."

"Can I get a gyro?"

After studying the brochure in the lobby of their accommodation, Erik and Baldwin decided to hike up one of the pinnacles near the monastery of Moni Megalou Meteorou. Near the base, they were fairly warm in the sheltered valley. As they ascended though, the wind blew through them and they were soon chilled. On the lee side of an outcrop, they snacked on almonds and a container of olives that Erik had squirrelled away in his light pack, a boost of energy to take them up the final ascent.

Noticing his son pensive demeanour, Erik put out a feeler. "And how are you today?"

"Cold. Like I'm wandering in the outer limits. No sunshine on offer."

"The sun will be back soon."

"Yes, but filtered by clouds."

"Perhaps you're forgetting something."

"What's that?"

"Perhaps the sun is happier when you're also a sun and you share the giving and receiving of sunlight. Then the situation is brighter."

"Mmm, yeah, right. I'll give it a try."

Erik nodded. "I think you'd be much happier, mentally, sharing energy—"

"Especially if there could be less clouds."

They set off again and ascended a number of switchbacks on the trail. Nearing the peak, they noticed footprints in the finely powdered gravel as the trail approached a crude metal structure on a concrete pad where cables had been strung to the neighbouring pinnacle, with the open carriage of a cable car gently swaying in the wind, creaking back and forth as it strained the wrought-iron anchor points where cable met seasoned wood.

It was very quick. Two men, now all too familiar, set on them. The first caught Erik in the back of the head with a stiff punch, sending him reeling face first into the open carriage where he slumped to the floor. Olof then smacked the brake on the car, sending it downward along the cable toward the opposite pinnacle. In the meantime, Baldwin was tripped from behind and punctured with a syringe in his neck, and a burlap bag put over his head. He was unconscious within seconds. Their luck had run out.

Olof and Dreadlocks took turns keeping Baldwin awake in the third-floor room of the Ameliana Hotel. He sat tied to a dining chair and slumped forward, his eyes bloodshot and unfocused. Each hour, the same questions were put to him:

"Do you want to see your father again?"

"What bank do you deal with?"

"Your father was awfully concerned about you — do you want us to describe what we've done to him?"

"What's your bank account code? If you tell us, we'll let your father go."

Baldwin remained silent. Those funds weren't just important to his own life — they were in part his mother's legacy and they'd help to fulfill his next dream, to get his father re-established in Flanders as part of his family once they returned home.

His only response was a flat reply. "Show me my father, then we'll talk."

Erik awoke in a dark cell. A monk with a long grey beard and an even longer black billowing robe had been tending to him since finding him in the cable car, bleeding from a lump on his head that had split after swelling. The cold wind and his slightly hypothermic condition had stifled the flow of blood, which the monk had treated once he had the blond man in the monastery infirmary. Parched, Erik swallowed some water that had been left at his bedside, then slowly sat up, his head pounding from even this small change in elevation.

The monk returned, this time carrying a tray with a bowl of soup. "You're looking better now … should I call you *Mijneer*? You're evidently Flemish from your papers."

"You are…"

"Call me Brother Demetrios."

"Brother … Demetrios, have you seen my son?"

"I have no idea about your son." The monk frowned. "And I'm sorry I had to look through your pack. I was very reluctant to pry. But we do have to be careful here that we're not harbouring criminals, so I had to look at your papers."

Erik nodded impatiently. He was far more interested in finding out what happened to Baldwin. "Fine, fine. I owe you a large thank-you for coming to my aid. But can you tell me, where exactly did you find me?"

"In the cable car. We thought you must have had an accident because there's no evidence you were robbed. We have kept all your belongings there, in that cabinet beside your bed. I can assure you we took nothing."

Erik turned, winced in pain as he lowered his head, and pulled open a small cabinet door. Inside, he pulled out his pack and verified the contents of his wallet and passport pocket, all there. But where was Baldwin? And who had hit him in the head?

Once his senses fully returned, he realized with dread who it was that would have attacked them, and his heart was immediately sick for the well-being of his son.

"I need to leave. I need to return to town."

"Please wait, you must not rush things. You need to regain your strength. Come now ... eat some of this soup."

He had a few spoonfuls, savouring the hearty broth, but then began to feel guilty. *The soup took too much time!* Erik thanked the monk profusely and then followed the exit signs to leave the monastery, his head pounding with each step.

Olof sent Dreadlocks out to look for the father, to drug him mildly and to bring him back to the hotel. They'd calculated at the time of the attack that it would take the two of them to whisk Baldwin down to the town and out of sight before the father recovered. It had been a good decision because they'd had just enough time to remove the bag from Baldwin's head before encountering another family of four hiking up who had offered help, which they quickly declined, saying their friend had twisted his ankle and they were taking him to the clinic. Dreadlocks had proceeded inside and opened the back door to the hotel to let in Olof, still carrying Baldwin, and to take him up the back stairs. In the lobby, Dreadlocks had passed an elderly couple. He stared at the husband briefly and then shook his head, still not confident that he didn't have a concussion from his dealings with his lunatic boss.

In the crisp air, Dreadlocks studied the village map and identified the pinnacle where the released cable car would have arrived with the father inside. Playing a hunch, he anticipated that the man would need to rest and recover if he awoke in the cold open car. He then set off up the slope at a quick pace hoping to catch him in convalescence at the monastery.

Baldwin tried to doze, but each time he did, he felt the rough rope tighten against his sore shoulders. Suffering through, he tried an experiment he'd used in church to amuse himself as a child. For about fifteen minutes, he stared over Olof's shoulder, offered a long blink and then an even longer yawn. He would repeat this every five minutes. After three efforts, he noticed that Olof's intense gaze started to lighten and drift off into a stifled yawn at first, but eventually into a full-fledged open-mouthed yawn. On noticing these, Baldwin had the presence of mind to slowly turn his head away before repeating the cycle in his best effort to cover up his pattern. Olof's head eventually became heavy and he drifted into a light doze. Seeing an opportunity, Baldwin worked his hands furiously in opposite directions, trying his best to loosen the cord that fastened his wrists to the back of the chair. He had enough play to start rubbing it against the end of a finishing nail that protruded at the base where a spindle met the lower rail.

Erik made his way down the switchbacks. His head had cleared, and though he missed out on most of Demetrios's soup, he'd finished off the olives and a crust of bread he'd left in his pack. The wind had not diminished, remaining fresh and chilled, leaving him thankful for the small woollen wrap that the kind monk had insisted he take with him. His thoughts were on Baldwin, which gave him additional adrenalin to keep moving. Seeing a familiar figure ascending around the next bend, he squatted down behind a display protruding from a recessed opening, a framed icon of the Virgin and Child covered in weathered plastic, replete with new and spent votive candles on each side. He pretended to tie his shoe, low to the ground with his back to the rock wall. Seeing his chance, he looked up and launched himself at Dreadlocks just as the young man had noticed he was not alone. Catching him with the palm of his hand under the chin, he quickly kicked the back of one knee and had the young man down and out of breath, one knee leaning on his groin, two hands clutching his throat. He shook and squeezed as the Spaniard gurgled and choked, then let off slightly.

"I'm going to let one hand go and you'll tell me where my son is! And if you struggle or lie to me, so help me God, I will choke the life out of you and pitch you over the side of this cliff with my bare hands, you little piece of shit!" For emphasis, he squeezed once more until Dreadlocks, now squealing in terror, nodded repeatedly.

He eased off, still ready to repeat if necessary. Gasping for air, the Spaniard attempted to speak. "Ho ... ho ... hotel."

"What hotel?"

"Ameli ... Ameliana."

Erik recalled the hotel from their entry into town. With a swift movement he undid and removed the Spaniard's belt, then dragged the man to his feet and wrapped the belt around his wrists behind his back. The younger man continued to fill his lungs with air to recover.

"Now, you're coming with me," Erik said. "What's your name?"

"Fabian."

"Family name?" Here Erik shook him vigorously to convey he wasn't taking any nonsense.

"Al ... Almanzar," he gulped out.

"Well, don't forget, Fabian Almanzar, any slip-ups and over the side you go."

Fabian stumbled ahead of the man. He didn't blame him. He would probably have done the same himself if it were his son, and in fact, he was willing to let this play out for the time being because he was more afraid of Olof than the man behind him.

Erik, his anger still on edge, could not help but notice his captive was just a bit older than his own son. "You're so young, Fabian. How did you get yourself involved with a guy like your partner? Is he the one that hit you in the eye?"

"Si ... yes, it's a long story."

"Try me. We have half a pinnacle to descend yet."

"So … what are we doing again, Mom?" asked Romy.

"We're changing hotels. We almost froze to death last night, and the topper was finding no hot water this morning. They'd a nerve asking for our endorsement for *Happy Planet*."

"Are we going to tell that annoying lady from New York we're leaving?" asked Guy.

"No, she was driving me nuts, asking a million silly questions and treating the restaurant people like they didn't know what they were doing just because their English was poor." Sadie felt little need to mince her words in explaining to the boys what was bad form when travelling.

"Yeah, she was a right numpty," Romy added.

It was an irritating noise — a repeated sound … pick, pick … pick, pick … like a mouse chewing behind a wall — that started to get to Olof as his cheek lay against the sleeve of his black jacket. Stirring slightly and opening his eyes, he noticed that the picking had stopped but that outside the room he was hearing a woman's voice speaking a Nordic language with a distinct central Asian accent that was familiar but completely out of context.

"Where could you have left it? We had everything from the train. I remember making sure so that we did not have any reason to spend one more minute with that awful girl."

"I don't know. I know that I brought it in with us, but the strap could have slipped from my wrist when we were signing in at the desk. We can look on our way out. It's only a small one and I'm sure they have others in the lobby for sale. Besides, it's too windy for an umbrella anyway."

"Well, I don't want too much sun and you know I'll never find a decent coiffeur in this little place. I'll look quite a sight!"

"So be it, dear, come on, get your shawl on and let's go."

"Have you seen the room key?"

When the two had quieted down, Olof heard again the familiar picking sound. He looked up and noticed the frayed ropes, and beyond that, stumbling to the door with the chair still attached to one leg, was the young Belgian, tearing away at the door locks. Olof whipped out a knife from his pocket and leaped toward his prisoner. Baldwin had the door open and swung it toward the onrushing Olof, catching his forward leg and causing him to stagger, knee burning in pain. Seeing the knife, Baldwin lurched with his wooden prison chair still clinging to his ankle toward the door handle of the adjoining room, simultaneously trying the knob and pounding on the door, screaming for them to call for help.

Immediately the neighbouring door was pulled wide open, the scene in the hallway turned black and white in all their minds. The furious figure of Fabian, fed up from abuse and having been released by Erik, leaped into the fray just as Olof lunged viciously at Baldwin with the knife. Fabian grappled Olof's knife arm, almost stabbing Baldwin's shoulder. Olof and Fabian fell askew and wrestled on the floor, fingers and thumbs gouging, no holds barred. Erik quickly jumped through the doorsill and stood on Olof's wrist as it lay flat, jarring his grip so the knife was released and skittered down the hallway toward the stairwell.

Now held down by Fabian, Erik and Baldwin, Olof was a grunting mass when the blond-haired boys and their mother ascended to the hallway from the landing below.

"Hey, Mom!" Romy shouted. "There's those ugly men again. They must be following us!"

Sadie jumped in front and swept the boys behind her, then kneeled down to pick up the knife at her feet.

Erik, still standing on the thug's arm, promptly yelled to her, "Pass me the knife!"

Trembling with fear and rage that her children had been put in danger again, and by the same men she thought were locked up from their terror in Turkey, she strode forward and passed Erik the knife handle first, then hurried back to her boys, taking them away from the scene, walking backward to avoid turning her back.

With the knife in Erik's hand hovering over the snarl of bodies on the floor, the extraordinary fracas was snapped from its spell by the foghorn bellowing of an enraged woman. "Olof! What on earth are you doing here? And with a knife? And how do these children know you? And … and … what kind of monster did that to your nose?"

Hearing his mother's voice, and feeling defeated and exhausted and with no further strength or weapon, Olof quit his struggle. Like the young Spaniard, he had reached a new low in his life and wasn't going to fight it anymore.

Baldwin and Erik sat quietly sipping iced coffees on the bus heading to Igoumenitsa on the west coast to catch the ferry to Bari, the port city just above the heel of the Italian boot. In their minds, Greece had provided them with some extraordinary travel experiences, some a bit too memorable, but balanced with the enrichment of time spent together they wouldn't trade for anything. Despite missing most of the Aegean Islands, Crete and the Peloponnese, they didn't feel like they gave the country short shrift. If anything, they knew that one day they'd go back to Thasos.

"And how will you fare in Italy after all that adventure? Still eager to go on?"

"Yes, definitely, as long as you're with me. We seem to enjoy the good bits and tackle the challenges very well together."

"Literally!" Erik chuckled. "And I think we share energy well, no?"

"Yes. That we do very well."

Near the back of the bus, an irritating voice could be heard. "You're Albanian? You don't sound like you're from Albany!"

PART 5

REPARATIONS

Father and son were nursing the tail end of their breakfast on a terrace in San Quirico d'Orcia, deep in the heart of Tuscany, both reflecting on the enjoyment of their small taste of the region. They'd spent the day previous touring Montalcino, appreciating a delightful lunch of characteristic Tuscan simplicity: thinly sliced prosciutto di Parma, shavings of pecorino cheese, small dishes of olives and roast peppers, all accompanied with baskets of the saltless Tuscan bread, Baldwin's medium for dipping in the tasty herb-infused oil and balsamic vinegar he spilled on his plate. The offering had been served in the open air under a cheerful pergola invaded by a tangle of grapevines. The sky above provided a perfect backdrop, clear and punctuated by sporadic puffs of cumulous cloud. Based on the glowing faces and ready smiles of the tour group, the mood was set for the true highlight: pre-poured carafes of delectable Brunello wine, a deep red made from only Sangiovese grapes and a source of pride for the local region. Following the meal, they'd gone for a walk to savour their experience and to take photos of the tall slender Cypress trees that adorned the rolling riot of greens and yellows of the countryside.

Perhaps it was the espressos over their breakfast, or maybe it was the pleasant but unfamiliar state of complete relaxation — the Italian dolce far niente — but father and son came out of their lull to have an animated discussion about their travel plans. Should they continue with laid-back leisure? Or was it time to take care of some unfinished business? Erik argued that their previous journey had been tainted with stressful criminal adventures that took away from their time together. He wanted to have some fun and enjoy the highlights of Europe.

Baldwin acquiesced to avoid belabouring the point and risk ruining their breakfast, but having experienced a nonstop immersion into the underworld of intrigue, he knew he wouldn't be able to truly relax until three boxes in his mind were checked: First, he wanted his father's name to be cleared of suspicion with regard to the missing funds from the family accounts; second, it was important to him that the criminal Augustus who looked to be directing their strife behind the scenes was taken out of circulation and presented to the police; and finally, there was another man in Istanbul who deserved his comeuppance, the criminal Funar Grigorescu, who had threatened not only Baldwin and Erik but also the tourist family from the UK with physical harm through his agent Olof Vintner. Baldwin still awoke during the night occasionally, sweating over the events.

No one was paying attention to their discussion though. There were other distractions for those breaking their fast outdoors, all under the watchful brain trust of the elderly locals sitting on the far side of the square on benches to share gossip and life's truths. This morning's spectacle included a young Canadian couple at a neighbouring table arguing vigorously, spitting insults to each other under their breath. She was tanned and wore a low-cut sundress to demonstrate the extent of how sun-kissed she was, with no less than a half dozen bangles chiming her every movement. Large round Gucci sunglasses pulled her ears out a bit further than she realized from her long wispy hair. She spoke with the corners of her mouth pursed, perhaps thinking it gave her an air of authority, although each thought voiced began with "like," which pricked that balloon. He looked as though he'd packed for their Italian holiday in fifteen minutes, wearing long cargo shorts, high-cut athletic shoes with laces untied and a collared bright-yellow golf shirt. To complete his fashion statement, he sported a baseball cap worn backward with a maple leaf logo, which leant the impression to Baldwin that it would be nailed to his head for all occasions. They'd been staying in the town over the previous three days and seemed omnipresent in both sight and volume. Their meal of fruit crêpes and whipped cream came to an abrupt end when she slapped him on the cheek, a clash of bangles punctuated by a smack heard across the courtyard. All nearby looked up suddenly as the force of the blow was palpable by the raised wheal on his face, soon taking on a distinct handprint below his temple. His cap had gone flying and landed beside Erik's foot. She then stormed off with her designer handbag, bangles jangling. The young man looked both shocked and apologetic as he collected the cap from Erik, who had leaned down from his chair to pick it up. He handed it to the man with a sympathetic half smile and raised eyebrows.

"Oh hey, like, sorry, man … thanks … er, *grazie*," the young man said as he accepted it.

Holding it in reverence, he put it back on his head, straightened the reversed peak obsessively, glanced at the table and, shaking his head with some embarrassment, went inside the café to pay the bill.

"They're even polite when they're angry," Erik chuckled, amused. "What's the saying? *Amor senza baruffa, fa la muffa* … 'love without a scuffle grows mould.'"

Baldwin laughed, in spite of the memory of the many heated discussions he'd had with his former girlfriend.

Their rough itinerary sketched out in the aftermath of this spectacle, they returned to their accommodation to pack.

"Did you send a text then?"

"Yes, to my contact in Istanbul. You may remember her, the veiled woman at the covered market."

"And did you mention the Roman coins?"

"Yes, but I had to be creative. The currency back then in this area was the salt itself, and I had to be sure to indicate the right Caesar!"

Erik and Baldwin spoke sotto voce with intermittent whispers. They were in the Salzkammergut region of Austria, poking around a gift shop. They'd just enjoyed the novelty of donning cotton coveralls, sitting on a burlap sack and sliding down a slippery wooden chute into the belly of a Roman-era salt mine, near Hallein. It was fascinating to see the tunnels where Celtic labourers had extracted blocks of salt over 2,600 years ago and to step farther along the passages into a primordial glow of lanterns revealing a shimmering subterranean lake. Baldwin was duly impressed and bought a postcard to send home to Tante Vivienne, while Erik made a brief call to his landlord in Thasos to explain that he would be away longer. On impulse, he also contacted Agent Costos to bring him up to date and to inquire who his local equivalent would be in the Salzburg region of Upper Austria.

They continued their chat in the car after leaving Hallein, enjoying the scenic views through the Salzkammergut Lakes District, passing by attractive rural Gasthofs catering to both the monied and those simply out for a country ramble. At a lookout high over the Wolfgangsee, near the village St. Gilgen, they took in the view.

"This area is so beautiful!" Baldwin said in wonder, his eyes shining.

"It is, isn't it?"

"You've been here before?"

"Yes, once, backpacking. A couple years before I met your mother. I travelled through the region and did one of those *Sound of Music* tours just to spend some time with some girls I'd met in a hostel in Salzburg. Then I took a train and went on my own to a small spa village, Bad Ischl."

"And how was that?"

"Well, in hindsight, a bit of a learning experience, really. There were very few young people in the spa, well … none, actually, and it killed my budget as the place I stayed in really wasn't meant for backpackers. There were mostly married people who I thought at the time were old wrinklies, and now I realize I'm probably as old as they were now," he said with a laugh.

"Wrinklies?" Baldwin laughed along.

"Yeah, I know. A bit mean, huh? That was then."

"So where to in Salzburg? What's there?"

"Well, first of all, the city is lovely just to have a walk around, the narrow streets have some interesting shops and we can do a tour of the Hohensalzburg Fortress, and then if we want to take a break we'll be spoiled for choice: there's the cafés along the Salzach River and another place I think you'll really enjoy. You'll know it when you see it." He grinned at his son. "I think I've come to know you over these last few months, it's more than a hunch."

"Okay then, let's go!" Baldwin smiled and moved to the car.

They made their way to Salzburg and found short-term lodging online along the Arenbergstrasse, a happy medium between the upscale hotels in the old town and the budget hostels Erik the Wrinkly expressly wanted to avoid. Crossing the river on the Karolinenbrücke to the old town centre, they wandered on foot as far as the old town hall and down to the splendour of the busy shopping street, Getreidegasse, all the while taking in the beautifully maintained Baroque architecture of Salzburg. The storied shops offered high-end fashion, jewellery, antiques and a wide assortment of epicurean delights. Above the pedestrian street, Baldwin looked up to see an array of traditional signs in wrought iron and gold, with German gothic script, each announcing the categories of treasures contained within their thresholds below. Numerous posters, T-shirts and other tourist tack featured Salzburg as the birthplace of the city's most famous celebrity, Wolfgang Amadeus Mozart, as if their shop in particular had been his favourite hangout, eschewing the crowd at the royal court.

"How are you doing?" Erik asked.

"I love this place! All these sweet shops and bakeries. I'm getting hungry."

"Very well, follow me, and we'll find something more substantial."

Baldwin followed his father past a number of restaurants on the Franz-Josef-Kai with open spots out front, but Erik stopped at none. Nor did he even glance at the menus, despite the entreaties of the formally aproned waiters patrolling among the tables hoping to catch their eye. The sun had climbed high in the sky, and the afternoon promised to be very warm. After fifteen minutes of walking, they were nearing the museum, and Baldwin, starting to sweat, became puzzled.

"Where are we going?"

"You wanted a nice meal."

"Yes, but we've already passed more than a half dozen places that looked good."

"Uh-huh."

"Why didn't we stop?"

"Patience."

"I'm starving and I'm getting hot." Baldwin was not happy not knowing the plan, but Erik only smiled. He liked to offer a surprise now and then, even if he had to deal with a bit of impatience.

They climbed the short rise north and turned a corner westward to bring Erik's target in view, the Augustiner Bräustübl, a former monastery built in the 1600s and in more recent times developed into a very popular sprawling restaurant and outdoor biergarten. From the noise of spirited diners and the smell of food emanating from the open rows of tables, Baldwin's eyes lit up in appreciation. They grabbed their own stone steins and lined up ready to receive their choice of beers straight from the barrel. Drinks in hand and straining their wrists, they found the end of a long table offered with a friendly half wave from an Irish couple who evidently had a head start, their steins cradled in hand and the leavings of their meal, including over half a basket of chips, still to be gathered by the wait staff.

Sitting down gratefully, they sipped their beers and looked around to catch the eye of anyone with an apron and a menu. The Irish fellow beside them had a friendly visage with a full beard. His bristly crop of dark hair looked to need no product to stick straight up to add an inch to his height. His wife had a pleasant smile, the highlight of her oval face. Her long dark hair was dead straight and shoulder length, and together with her flowing dress and tall boots, she had the appearance of the lead singer of a folk band.

"I see you got your drinks in then. That's a good start," the fellow said in a pleasant, lyrical manner.

"Yes, I have a feeling the first one won't last long, a bit of a walk over here in today's sun," Erik replied.

After all the hiking he and Baldwin had done, Erik felt a bit sheepish coming up with this lame comeback just to acknowledge the friendly gesture offered, but he smoothed it over quickly with a question. "Been here in town long?"

"Just arrived today. We started in Munich, setting there in the *Hofbrauhaus* doing the same thing we're doing here … Oh wait, I'm afraid we're not giving you a good impression, are we?" The man laughed at his own joke. His wife just smiled and shook her head slightly. "Then we went up to see the Eagle's Nest in Berchtesgaden where the wee corporal villain with the toothbrush moustache hung out back in the day. And we're off to Vienna tomorrow."

"That sounds like a great tour," Erik said, turning to bring in Baldwin, who was still looking around for a waiter.

"I'd say the lad's hungry," said the woman.

The waiter had not yet dropped off a menu, and Baldwin was beginning to feel the first of his beer stirring in his head. "Oh, I'm fine," he said a little self-consciously. At eighteen, he was still a bit shy when an attractive woman singled him out.

"Well, here then anyway," she said, sliding the basket of chips over. "Have at these. I've been watching you eye them up, and sure as God's got sandals, I'll not be needin' them."

"Oh, thank you!" said Baldwin, tucking three in his mouth before coming up for air.

A middle-aged waiter came around a corner, immediately perceptive in watching the dynamics at the table, and dropped off two menus. Erik was quick to stop him from leaving again, raising a finger, and ordered after only a quick glance at the thick menu set out in multiple languages.

"*Bitte, zwei portionen schweinshaxen mit kartoffelsalat.*"

"*Sehr gut,*" offered the waiter, and then confirmed the orders in Dutch, holding up two fingers. "*Twee bestellingen?*"

"*Ja, alstublieft,*" Erik confirmed appreciatively. "This guy has a good eye," he said to Baldwin, gesturing to his small rucksack with the embroidered Belgian flag. Tante Viv's handiwork strikes again!

"What did you order? Baldwin asked.

"Oh, the the pork knuckles, of course." Erik grinned. "Comes with potato salad."

The Irish laughed and Baldwin smiled. He'd had them before and knew them to be a load of delicious but greasy, heavy food. He didn't care today. He was really hungry.

They made light chatter with the Irish couple about their favourite chips versus Flemish *frieten* and amiably decided to agree to disagree regarding who best treated the popular tuber native to neither land, brought over rather from the New World. Another round was contemplated, but the Irish couple begged off to go for a walk. They wished each other well and safe travels just as Baldwin and Erik were finishing the last of what they could finish of the huge portions.

"Well, now we have friends in Galway." Baldwin imitated the Irish lilt.

"Next trip," Erik replied. He was about to laugh but checked himself, blowing out air, remembering how full he was and that he didn't want to tempt fate.

After going for a short walk themselves, they booked a tour for the morning to see the Hohensalzburg Fortress, and then split a small strudel at a riverside café, going over their strategy for the next day, which included a bit of business.

"*Grüss Gott* … er, good morning. Is this Pichler? Tobias Pichler?" A voice with an accent rang up.

"*Ja*, who is this calling?"

"I'm Agent Athanasios Costos from Athens. We met in Venice."

"The … oh, *ja*, the Museums Council discussion, at the Europol meeting … umm, *ja* … I remember. Over lunch you were telling the story of coins stored in a stuffed monkey."

Agent Tobias Pichler was a large man, over two metres in height and with a stout build that was daunting to many of the suspects he interrogated. He also had challenges in clothing shops finding bargain rate plaids and stripes suitable for his frame. To be back in uniform would have been a blessing. But he was his own man and wore what he felt comfortable with, which meant rumpled gabardine trousers and a fashion-challenged cardigan with elbow patches. He had a round face, an army-grade brush cut of greying hair and a thick moustache he trimmed on occasion. His large hands, with a grip that would be the envy of a stevedore, held a cigarette the majority of his day, making them appear even larger.

"That's me, yes," Costos said.

"*Ja*, how can I help you?"

Half an hour later, Pichler finished his lunch of Wiener Würstchen in a biergarten just outside of Linz, inserted his latest cigarette end into the dregs of his can of Stiegl and thought about his conversation with the Greek, Costos. Pulling out his mobile, he rang to brief a colleague on a lead for the next day.

"What did you think of the fortress?" Erik asked.

"It was interesting. Maybe it was the translations, but the tour was less detailed than one I took for the Gravensteen in Ghent, but hands down, the scenery and the lookout over the city was fantastic and has Ghent beat there."

"We're from what's called the Low Countries for a reason."

"I know, but you asked."

"I did."

"And, I know one other thing."

"What?"

"Being tortured and then thrown down an oubliette would suck."

"Yes."

Retracing their steps through the old city, they returned via the narrow Judengasse — the Jewish Quarter until the late 1400s, but more recently, a street of quaint shops without synagogues or Jewish schools — the name and the odd doorway the only visible legacy. They then proceeded across the river, made their way to the railway station and sat for a coffee.

"You ready?"

"Yes," Baldwin said. "We need to do this."

"We only have a grainy photo to go by."

"But you've heard their accent?"

"Barely. Once or twice, a recorded phone call."

"Can I ask a question?"

"Of course."

"What does a Romanian look like?" Baldwin looked sheepish for a moment.

"Oof … you may as well ask what a Belgian looks like. For one thing, in the old pre-WWI Austro-Hungarian Empire, there were a mix of Hungarians, Germans, Poles, Serbs, Slovaks, Saxons, Jews, Romani and a half dozen others that had settled in Transylvania, even Tatars and Armenians, which we wouldn't necessarily think of being there. And when the post-WWI treaties assigned Transylvania and other areas to Romania, it almost doubled their land area." He shook his head. "Those treaties were a shambles."

"What do you mean?"

"The Paris conference was — well, let's just say, some slick presenters walked away with undeserved lands, and other deserving peoples came away almost empty handed, depending on who was paying attention and who was hung over. That pompous prick Wilson didn't help either, but that's another story."

"You sound really angry," Baldwin said, noting the colour rising in his father's face.

"Well, just for one, Flanders — our land — when it was a medieval county, was once much larger than it is now, but it was passed around … It would seem because of our location and landscape, anyone could conquer us, but the important thing is, no one could rule us because we had brains of our own. We were leaders in the Northern Renaissance. My point is, Belgium deserved a better outcome as the battlefield of Europe, but I don't want to go on about this. Suffice to say, Romania has the legacy of many different peoples, and a Romanian could take many shapes and forms. We need to be sure, though, on the appearance and identity of *our* man."

Erik felt like he went on a little too strong but noticed that his son seemed to be teeming with pride. A few moments later, Baldwin mused that he was looking forward to reading more about the historical dynamics of his homeland and less about the crusading ventures of noblemen.

When the late-evening train from Vienna was ten minutes from the station, Baldwin left out the main door and headed in the twilight to a bench near the parking area behind the station, seeing in the back row a curiously small Volkswagen up! occupied by a very large man. Erik remained in the café, hovered over a dog-eared copy of *Die Ganze Woche* looking nonchalant and sipping a long espresso he'd nursed for twenty minutes. He read through the photo captions trying to make sense of the glossy tabloid, but his mind was not in it, and he was certainly out of his element on the topic of celebrities. To complete his look to blend in, he wore a battered short-style Tyrolean hat with a red feather he'd bought in the Hallein shop, aging it prematurely by stepping on it a few times and puffing it back out. By his side was Baldwin's rucksack with its small Belgian flag displayed on top of the opening flap. Below the rucksack was a small flat wooden box with a latch. Hearing the second notice of arrival of the Vienna train, he placed the box within the magazine, pushed it to the corner where it would be easily seen and then waited.

Funar Grigorescu was irritated that he had to leave Istanbul. When he had to travel, he did so under one of his false passports to meet his contact Augustus, usually at neutral locations. Always a warehouse, never a bar or restaurant. *He's such a cheapskate!* Funar thought. On this occasion it was a different matter. He'd initially rejected outright the entreaties of Beyza Aydin, his intriguing Istanbul business acquaintance, to collect on her behalf her recent acquisition of illicit coins in Vienna. She'd begged him to go because her Schengen visa application had been delayed. Funar's assumption remained unvoiced — that she had failed in an attempt to bribe a notary to provide the stamp.

He didn't do business with Beyza often, but when he did, it was always memorable as they typically ended up in bed for a vigorous session. Her veiled, conservative dress was merely a front for the determined tigress beneath who knew how to manipulate the aging felon. The liaisons were never when he requested, always on her terms. Under her request, which quickly took the tone of instruction, he'd flown to Vienna, this time as the German businessman, Franz

Gregory. Landing in Vienna, he'd contemplated checking into a hotel near the airport when he received a text from Beyza that he would need to proceed by train to Salzburg.

He replied back, again annoyed. *I want 500€ more.*

You'll get what I give you, she wrote back, *and you'll get what I give you very well.*

Okay, I'm here now in Austria, he thought. She said she would provide more detail in due course. He replied, *How will I know courier?*

The delay in her response was pointed, reminding him who was in charge: *chk ur phone in Salzburg, only then*

"She's such a control freak," he muttered and shook his head, wondering where his common sense went when it came to dealing with her. Then he remembered their last exertions together, and he took a taxi to the Vienna Central Station to catch the evening train west.

"You're the Belgian?" Agent Pichler asked.

"One of them."

"There are more?"

"My father is inside."

"Okay, let's go."

"Just you, is it?"

"Am I not enough?" Agent Pichler said, eyes twinkling, pointing to himself in laconic humour.

Baldwin could see he was a formidable presence. He accompanied Agent Pichler in through a side door to the station, and they headed for the café.

The Vienna train pulled into the station at Salzburg. Shaking off the doze of train travel, Funar quickly checked his phone. As if his progress was being watched, a text arrived: *Courier in caf. Alp hat w red feather. Small pack Belg flag. Take magasine n txt me. Box within. Once I answr, leave. ovrnght back to Vienne.*

Quite cryptic, he thought. What about payment? He replied, *Pmt arranged?*

The reply reflected her characteristic impatience. She did business like she had sex. *Arrangd. Don't fck up.*

Funar exited the train and made his way along the platform. He was sporting his version of travel wear: a threadbare olive-coloured suit with a white shirt yellowing around the collar and unbuttoned almost halfway so his pelt of chest hair threatened to burst out. Desert-brown suede slip-ons, a well-worn trilby and a battered leather briefcase completed the look of a hard-working salesman. He entered the Salzburg train station and glanced around for any signs of police or security. There seemed to be none. He then proceeded to the newsstand and pretended to glance through the *Tiroler Tageszeitung* while he looked for the locations of security cameras. He put the paper back, to the annoyance of the aging Arab woman behind the counter, and proceeded to the café.

"What do you mean he changed his password?" Augustus barked, annoyed.

"Just what I said, he's changed it, his PIN code, and I can't help you any further."

"You'll help me, or I'll deal with your fine French beauty the same way I dealt with the other old fool."

"Walloon ... but, what can I do?"

"Look, *arschloch* ... you already received your cut, so you'll find a way!"

The line disengaged. Remi tossed his mobile on the passenger seat of his car and resumed chewing his thumbnail while trying to think of an excuse to use Old Viv's phone again.

Funar entered the café and, seeing the Tyrol hat and travel pack, approached Erik, who looked up slowly. Funar walked past, and with a barely perceptible nod, picked up the magazine from the edge of the table beside the empty espresso cup, tucked it under his arm and headed for the door. Back in the main hall, he glanced up at the board for the next train to Vienna, and then noticed an extremely large man with a bushy moustache walking toward him. There was no mistaking that he represented the local authorities. Fear kicked in, and Funar, eyes wide with panic, bolted away from the giant toward the main doors of the station and bumped into a young blond fellow who, expecting such an interaction, drew up a stiff elbow. Funar staggered from the blow to his face, nearly tripping, when two stout men in dark-coloured jackets seized him by the arms. The wooden box hidden within the magazine slipped out and cracked loudly when it hit the shiny tiled floor. A small cache of a dozen or so ten- and twenty-cent coins rolled and scattered toward the news agent. Seeing who was apprehended, the Arab woman behind the counter smiled. She picked up her mobile to call her daughter to relay her evening's victory.

Agents Tobias Pichler and Athanasios Costos questioned Funar Grigorescu for over two hours. There were sweat stains under the arms of Funar's jacket, and the odour in the small interview room of the police station defied the ventilation settings to clear the air. They already had his correct identity from their undercover contact in Istanbul, a very capable Armenian woman who used numerous aliases, including Beyza Aydin.

"We need a little more cooperation, Funar." Costos was leading the questioning, his hands down on the table, leaning in so that Funar could smell the coffee on his breath.

"I'm Franz Gregory. I've told you all I know. That bitch in Istanbul set me up. What more can I say."

"Enough with the Franz shit, Funar. You don't seem to understand how much trouble you're in." Costos pushed off the table and began pacing around it. "False passport, false Schengen visa, before even mentioning how many museum heists we have you linked to." Costos turned and faced Funar again. "You need to come clean on your contacts."

The room suddenly felt smaller to Funar, perhaps it was a headache coming on, squeezing his head from within. Either way, his answers became more flippant, borderline desperate. "You're fishing. I have no contacts to give."

"We want the Deutscher. Give him to us and with evidence and we can discuss some concessions."

"I know no German in antiquities."

"Funar, Funar, Funar … I have Bucharest on speed dial and your photo already attached to a draft email. They've been after you for years. You've read about Romanian prisons … I've heard they like fresh pork in there. Here piggy, piggy, piggy. So out with it!" Costos shouted in his ear. "Who is your contact?"

"*Du-te dracului!*" he cursed in his native tongue. "You have nothing on me."

The dog-eared copy of the thick *Die Ganze Woche* magazine suddenly reappeared on top of his head, accompanied by the slam of a monstrous fist, sending a bolt of pain down through his spine.

"Wrong answer, Franz Funar!" barked the giant with the moustache.

The room smelled worse. Funar had soiled his pants.

Augustus Krauledat drove a rusty brown Volkswagen van across the Bendorf Bridge, crossing the Rhine north of Koblenz in the west of Germany. He felt his seventy-three years and cursed his new vehicle, a necessary purchase since his faithful Barkas B 1000 cracked an axel, overloaded with a shipment of concrete. He tossed his empty KARO cigarette pack out the driver's window and reached into the glove box for another pack. It was 4:00 a.m. and he'd not slept for twenty-five hours, leaving Leipzig late the previous morning after receiving an urgent text, one that he perceived would threaten to unravel his whole network. The source was his weakest link. *Trier. 0600. Christof Hotel Café.*

In part to stay awake, Augustus spoke softly to himself. "Trier? What can be so urgent? And why the fuck Trier of all places? He drinks only beer, no wine, and is too stupid to care about the Roman empire or the First Reich or to attend a university. He must be sniffing around the young girls there again, the filthy rat. I should have never taken him there."

Augustus was a survivor, his family tree a tale of struggle and tragedy. As a young toddler, and later a growing boy, Augustus grew used to his father, Vytautus, cuffing him and slapping his mother, Raisa. Vytautus spent most of his time carousing with the rough SA crowd, culminating one night in November of 1938, when many of the shops in his native Allenstein, East Prussia, were severely damaged, including the haberdashery of his wife's family.

That November evening, Vytautus arrived home drunk and cursing the stain of the *Juden* on his life. Shocked and resigned at his behaviour, Raisa appealed to her father-in-law, Armonis, then fled to the bedroom, taking Augustus and his sister with her. Armonis stood ready when Vytautus appeared at the door.

"Hey, Papa," Vytautus crowed, weaving. "You should see the clever Juden family Lewin now! They ran away cowering today. Now I won't have to put up with the nasty comments in the streets behind my back. Where's the *Schlaue Jüdin* anyway? Where are the kids?"

"I heard what you did. You would hang your head in shame if you had any brains," Armonis said.

"They're scum. They take our money, they—"

Armonis cut him off and cut him down. "It's you who take their money, *dummkopf.* Raisa's family have been there for us numerous times when we have come up short on this farm. But you forget this conveniently, you and your drunken Worker Party swine buddies. You have two lovely children and a beautiful wife and you waste all of our money in town. Your mama would be so disappointed to see who you have turned into — a no-good, slovenly wifebeater."

Vytautas's face turned from self-satisfied bluster, to disbelief, to a vicious sneer within moments. He came at his father, who was ready with his hardwood cane. Armonis, gauging his timing well, gave his son a swift downward crack just beside his right ear, painfully tearing the tendon and separating his shoulder. Vytautus screamed as he shrunk to his knees, his right arm limp and on fire. Raisa and the two young children emerged from the bedroom to see him holding his right arm in his left, screaming obscenities at his father. Augustus followed his mother and sister out the door, each with a suitcase. He looked with sad bewilderment at his father. They would join his mother's family that evening in Königsberg, only returning to the farm and to Opa Armonis two months later, once they heard that Vytautus had joined the Wehrmacht and was training at the Kriegsschule in Dresden.

During the first week of December 1941, Augustus learned that his father had perished, frozen in the mud and snow twenty kilometres from Moscow. His mother's family had returned to Allenstein from Königsberg, and Raisa and her daughter were quietly running their shop while Augustus attended school. In early 1942, his mother and sister were collected and deported along with most of the Allenstein Jewish community to a ghetto in Minsk. His Opa Armonis knew that time was not on Augustus's side. The industrious old man had new papers prepared for his grandson, bribing a local photographer to prepare them in the name of Augustus Krämer, to allow him to join, underaged, the Hitlerjugend. At the end of the war, Augustus burned the papers with his new identity. Once again, he was a Krauledat.

Decades later, Augustus Krauledat smoked another KARO and glanced again at the text. *Trier. 0600. Hotel Christof Café.*

Not much to go on, he thought, annoyed. He didn't want to have to call the little Belgian prick who was dragging him this far from home.

They sat in Tante Vivienne's kitchen, glasses charged, sharing a bottle of the sweet muscatel she was fond of sipping in the evening, her discovery from a trip to Spain long before the waffle trade took over her life.

"Where's Remi?" Vivienne asked Yvonne.

"On the road again. When it's not for the *chemin de fer*, it's for one of his side businesses — you know the ones he tells me nothing about."

"What kind of business?" asked Vivienne.

"Spare parts ... so he claims," replied Yvonne. "Parts for what, I don't know. He's not at the mill anymore since Etienne passed. I know it's not for drugs at least, he's putting on a bit of weight and I know he wouldn't have the discipline not to try them himself."

"Oh dear, I wish Baldwin were back. He could talk to him, straighten him out."

"*Oui* ... me too..."

Close questioning of Funar Grigorescu revealed that his German contact, one Augustus Krämer, would be in Trier ostensibly to meet with a young Belgian operative. The arrangement was straightforward. Agents Costos and Pichler would be on hand to take in Krämer. The Belgian father, Erik, and his son, Baldwin, would be brought in to identify the young Belgian who was linked to the underworld network — the same underworld network connecting Istanbul to Greece, but also linking Istanbul to Leipzig, and Leipzig to Zeebrugge. Baldwin had heard a general description of the young Belgian and hoped it was not who he anticipated it might be when he heard that the German had been dealing with an elderly Belgian who had dropped out of contact suddenly.

They'd all been driven overnight from Salzburg in a black Mercedes S-Class limousine and now pulled into a service station outside of Trier at 5:30 a.m. for a rest stop and coffee.

"What's the plan?" asked Erik, wincing as he drank a roadside espresso.

"They're to meet at the café of the Hotel Christof," Costos replied. "We proceed into town, park in the Mercure hotel, pull in opposite the black gate — and then we wait and watch for a brown VW van."

Remi Zwaenepoel crossed Luxembourg into Germany as the sun began to dawn. He glanced again at the puzzling text. *0600. Christof Hotel Café. Trier.*

Not much to go on, he thought, annoyed. He didn't want to have to call the old German prick who apparently was his contact now since old Etienne had bit it. It didn't make sense that communications had bypassed Decroos, Etienne's old buddy who had gotten them into all this, but nothing had been clear from the start with this lot of crooks.

Remi stayed the night in Arlon, as he had in past, to save money before entering Luxembourg and Germany. As usual, he had a cheap dinner of steak frites at the Café au Beurre before heading to his lodgings — an apartment owned by the rather dim Hélène, a waitress he'd met in a bar one late night when old Augustus took him to Trier. Remi liked her curves, her easiness and the fact that she didn't care when he was coming back again. It didn't occur to him that she may have the same approach with others. From the state of her apartment, and especially her shower, it was plain that she didn't host often, but for Remi, it was more about quantity than quality.

At 6:00 a.m. in Trier, Agent Costos noticed a beater of a Volkswagen van with shit-brown paint rumble into town and park in an alley off one of the commercial buildings in the old city square. He left the hotel with Erik, picked up a newspaper, and the two entered the Christof. In the café, Costos ordered them both an espresso to provide relief from the roadside nonsense they suffered earlier in the morning. They sat at a table along the window, a back portion of the paper handed to Erik for perusal. Erik rolled his eyes and executed the scripted instructions he'd been given, proceeding to gripe in low tones about the salaries of professional footballers.

Over the non-conversation, both men watched an old fellow walk in and look around. Wearing a surplus-store East German military jacket, with his left hand in his pocket, he had the air of someone who didn't want to be there, who despised the whole premise behind high-end Italian coffee, and if it weren't for expanding his network, someone who was regretting the day the wall came down in Berlin. He found a table in the corner and sat staring at the door. His entry was followed by the emergence of a young stocky fellow with thick dark hair slicked back and wearing a long checkered flannel shirt and torn denim jeans. Roach-killer cowboy boots completed the look as he ambled into the café, looking even more out of place than the septuagenarian who was watching for him.

According to plan, Erik sent a text to Baldwin to proceed to the café. If he knew the young contact, he was to pretend it was coincidental and invite the fellow to join him later for a beer, knowing this would irritate the old one.

Five minutes later, Baldwin walked into the café and up to the counter to order, pointing discreetly to the table of his father, then turned his head with nonchalance to take in the clientele. Remi was drinking coffee with an old fellow at a table in the corner. His childhood friend stared at him with a look of confused disbelief and muttered something to the old fellow. Baldwin, inwardly disappointed that his friend had put his ladder on the wrong wall, feigned surprise and, putting on a fake smile, walked over to the table.

"Hey, man! This is whacked! *Hoe gaat 't met je?* How are you here now?"

"Just for a quick meeting with someone from work." Remi nodded toward Augustus, but then pointedly turned away from him to keep the conversation directed at Baldwin.

Deep down, Baldwin wanted to give Remi at least the chance to explain, but it was not to be. Remi noticed the look on the face of the old fellow at the table as he glanced back, a look of extreme annoyance, and he felt caught between his reason to be there and his surprise at seeing Baldwin appear from nowhere.

"How's Yvonne?" Baldwin asked.

"Good. Asks constantly if I've heard from you," Remi said, with a bit of an edge to his voice.

This light banter was too much for Augustus, who smelled a rat. He tossed a five-euro note on the table. Another source of annoyance. He preferred the deutschmark and didn't yet trust the new euro. *Why couldn't they leave things alone?*

"I drove all night to get here," he barked out. "Call me later when you're done, *dummkopf.*"

He rose and briskly left the café. He was barely five paces from the door when a huge man with a moustache intercepted him.

"Ahh, Herr Krämer, I believe ... a moment of your ti—"

Pichler never finished his sentence. Augustus pulled his hand out of his pocket and pepper-sprayed Agent Pichler full in the eyes, then took off at a hurried trot toward the alley where his van was parked. Pichler's face turned red as he gasped for air, wiping with the back of his fists at his eyes, which burned and watered. He pulled out a handkerchief, coughed and tried to see in which direction his assailant had gone.

Inside the café, Remi was sheepish in his conversation. "Wow, crazy! I didn't expect to see you here!"

"Me neither. Sorry to interfere with your meeting. That was a business meeting, you said?"

"Sort of ... it's complicated. How are your travels? Where've you been?"

"My coffee order is up. I'll get it to go. Come with me and we can catch up."

Baldwin paid, glanced at his father and Costos, and took his coffee with him as he and Remi left the café.

Outside, he noticed to his left that Agent Pichler was struggling with tears in his eyes, his runny nose left a disgusting mess in his moustache, and he was coughing while being helped by a uniformed police woman, her brunette hair gathered at the back under her cap. Steering clear, Baldwin's mood turned. Boyhood loyalties kicked in. He held Remi's arm and made for a small grove of trees to their right on the far side of the square, hidden from view of the Christof by some raised flower beds and the Roman Porta Nigra itself.

"Why the big hurry?"

"Quick, are you involved with something criminal?"

"Well, no, not exactly ... with people who might be though ... well, kind of, why? What's this got to do with you? You're on holiday!"

"Get out of here. Leave. Now. I'll tell them you were lured here by mistake in place of another. Just trust me. There are Europol agents. Leave now!"

Remi gave him a puzzled look, but saw he was sincere. "Thanks, man. I can explain." But no other words came out of his mouth. He just turned and walked away to leave the precinct of the Roman Black Gate.

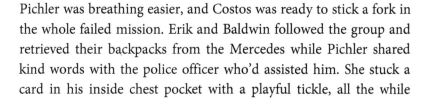

Erik and Agent Costos paused for two minutes after Baldwin left with the Slickster and followed them out of the café. Once outside, they noticed to their left a bleary-eyed and coughing Agent Pichler sitting on the rear bumper of a Stadtpolizei vehicle. He was accompanied by a stout-looking policewoman squatting in front of him, offering soothing words and repeated ministrations of saline solution to the grateful giant. She had rushed over to nearby optometrist in the shopping district for help and been back with a bottle of relief in admirable time.

"Pichler, what happened?" Costos asked.

Pichler blew his nose and wiped his moustache with his handkerchief for the twelfth time.

"The old one sprayed me with the pepper shit and got away." This led to repeated throat clearing and more wiping. "Don't even ask me about the other one with the hair."

Erik noticed Baldwin was returning on his own. He looked at Erik intently. "It wasn't him. It was … Jakob."

He was a poor liar, but Agent Costos was too concerned with Agent Pichler to pick up on it. Erik could see through the nonsense. He knew Baldwin was protecting Remi and had his reasons, even if they weren't well placed at the moment.

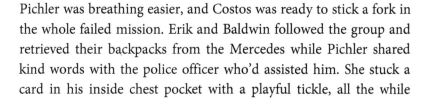

Pichler was breathing easier, and Costos was ready to stick a fork in the whole failed mission. Erik and Baldwin followed the group and retrieved their backpacks from the Mercedes while Pichler shared kind words with the police officer who'd assisted him. She stuck a card in his inside chest pocket with a playful tickle, all the while wondering what year his jacket was actually in fashion.

"We'll stay for the day and catch a train to the Belgian coast tomorrow," said Erik. "If you need anything further from us regarding the East German, uh … Krämer, let us know. You have my number."

The implication was that they were finished in their police adventures and could resume their travels.

"So what did the guy with the slick hair say to you? The young man?" persisted Costos, now with full attention back on mission.

"He doesn't seem to be involved. I mean, he was sent by someone … Dupuy? D'Hondt, DeBruyne? D-something … some former employee of my late uncle, that much I got."

Erik's brain was beginning to stretch as far as the bogus story. Baldwin had just thrown a handful of West Flanders family names into the mix. Had he added a *Van* something, it might have raised the percentage to half. He picked up his pack and made motions for them to leave the Europol agents to the work of picking up the trail of the East German who was at the core of their investigation.

Augustus was fuming as he raced back eastward, approaching the Bendorf Bridge over the Rhine north of Koblenz. "Goddamn little Belgian prick. Goddamn Austrian cop. Goddamn Dago sidekick or whatever the fuck he was, and GODDAMN FUNAR! I only meet one good person in my life and I'm forty years too late!"

He looked in the rearview mirror and saw flashing lights. He'd had enough racing his old beater on the autobahn at this point and took the exit. In four minutes, having lost the flashing lights, he drove into Waschi Waschi Auto, turned off the car and took all the paperwork from the glove box. There was no cargo of value, and the van irritated him anyway, so off he went, dressed in an East German jacket, determined to lie low again. *Perhaps someday*, he thought as he walked to the local train in Engers, *I will look up that clever fraulein, Violet Beret, and pass her the key for the locker at the Leipzig station and the envelope hidden there so she can enjoy the life, even if I cannot.*

On Friday of that same week, Baldwin and Erik stepped off the train in Bruges to a mini family reunion. Tante Vivienne ran up to give Baldwin a huge hug, swinging him around such that his backpack sent a stanchion flying across the platform. Oncle Marcel at first enjoyed the spectacle and then stared at his brother, Erik. Tears soon came to his eyes at seeing this younger version of himself from a time too long past. Erik equally teared up and gave his older brother a big hug. He turned to Vivienne to do the same as Baldwin hugged his uncle. Over Oncle Marcel's shoulder, he noticed Yvonne. He ran to her, picked her up and swung her around. Collecting himself, he looked around. The rest of the onlookers on the platform were strangers, yet all appreciated the display of love reunited.

"What happened?"

"I had enough."

"Enough of what?"

"The lies, the unexplained work trips, the thievery, the Café au Beurre and someone named Hélène."

"What lies?" Baldwin asked.

Yvonne shook her hair off her shoulders. "He would borrow your Tante Vivienne's phone, sweet-talking her into revealing her passwords, and he found a document with the code for one of your accounts and for the safe at the mill."

"Wait, Tante Vivienne wrote down my passcodes? Thank God I kept to myself the code for the main account!"

"Oh don't blame her. She's all thumbs and probably couldn't keep everything straight, so she turned to—"

"Remi, of course," he cut off her thought.

"Yes, Remi. And I found out he was working with some criminals. I don't know how he got involved with them. But it turns out they were the same criminals who were involved in taking fifteen thousand francs from the mill about twenty years ago. Some *connard stupide* called Decroos. This was the money your Oncle Etienne accused your father of taking before he left for France. Later they were trying to get at your money from Oncle Marcel."

"What did you mean by the Café au Beurre?"

"Remi came home two days ago, drunk out his mind, muttering something about you saving his skin in Trier. I found a receipt in the front pocket of his shirt before I threw it in the wash. It was from Arlon. A meal for two. I phoned the restaurant and of course they remembered the loud Fleming in high spirits, in with a busty beauty named Hélène. When he woke up, I asked where his hotel bill was. I asked where the café bill was. He said he lost them and just stormed out to the pub, yelling that I don't trust him, blah, blah, blah."

"Where is he now?"

"He came back early yesterday morning, packed a small bag with his wallet, put on his stupid pointy boots and left with our car."

"What car? Still the blue Peugeot?"

"Yes."

"Do you know the licence plate number?"

"Sure. It's an old-style red one, KVL321."

Baldwin was now extremely annoyed with himself for giving Remi the benefit of the doubt in Trier. He knew the agents pressed hard and he believed that sometimes they wouldn't stop short of stitching someone up to get at their contacts. But now he'd lost all respect for his childhood friend and didn't care to see him ever again.

A week later, Baldwin sat with his father and Oncle Marcel at the Café Zonnebloem. During a break from the waffle stand, Tante Vivienne came over to join them.

"So Remi was located? By whom, Pichler?" asked Erik.

"Yes, Agent Pichler."

"Pichler looked to be in good hands when we left him," Erik said smiling.

"Yes, he was the happiest man I've ever seen who'd just been pepper-sprayed … that said, he's the only man I've ever seen who's been pepper-sprayed … I gave him the plate number for Yvonne's Peugeot. It didn't take long. They pulled Remi over just outside of Mouscron. He was heading for Lille."

"Did you know Lille is a Flemish city? Before Louis IV, it was Rijsel," Erik said in earnest.

"Oh yes, Flemish," added Oncle Marcel. "It's where our name Van Ryssel came from. From Rijsel."

"Seriously?" Tante Viv put in, "I wouldn't know that you two jokers and Etienne were brothers."

"Not at all," laughed Baldwin.

Tante Viv looked reflective. "So you're going back to Greece soon?" she asked Erik. "We just have you back finally."

"Well, I … have my business there … and now that the issue with Etienne, God forgive his soul, is resolved … what can I do? This is something I'd really have to think about with Baldwin now."

"Papa," Baldwin replied, his face earnest, "you have your business and a beautiful place there on Thasos, a life there that you know. You also know that you have a place here. If you're worried about me, don't. I've decided to enrol in university, in business and commerce, specializing in—"

"Antiquities!" his father blurted out, laughing.

"Yes!" Baldwin gushed. The whole table laughed.

"I believe you'll have a leg up on most in your class!" There was laughter in Erik's eyes as he put his arm around Baldwin's shoulders.

EPILOGUE

THIS LIFE

Baldwin and Yvonne spoke softly to each other as they sat on a bench overlooking the narrow canal outside of Damme. It was four in the morning. A full moon provided enough light to see the canal waters and the whole countryside with a beautiful blue-grey hue. They shared the quiet, interrupted every few minutes or so by a persistent cricket chirping. The chirping stopped, as if in answer, giving them a minute of silent respite, each to their own feelings.

He picked up her hand and kissed it, held it in his and pulled her over into his lap. "You're coming with me then, on your school breaks, when I'm doing field research?"

"Where would we go for this fieldwork?" she asked.

"Well, to Thasos in Greece to see my father, and then to join Baldwin the Crusader in Veliko Tarnovo."

"Hmm, yes, I read your postcard from there."

The cricket started and stopped after a few moments.

"I feel you."

"And I feel you."

"And…"

"And what?"

"And we don't need another life!"

Printed in the USA
CPSIA information can be obtained
at www.ICGtesting.com
JSHW011102221124
74101JS00002B/3

9 781771 807135